UNDERSTANDING ADAM

DR K. LUBEET

ISBN: 9798840038420

CONTENTS

1

A QUIET NEED.

The gentle yet rhythmic shaking of the bed woke me from my slumber. I tensed slightly, my senses quickly alerting me that something was going on in my bed. Something that I hated, something repulsive, sickening even. I lay in wait, listening intently, staring into the darkness of the night. Ready to pounce!

#

The slight motion created by her awakening alerted Adam. He lay still, holding his breath trying to control his heart rate. His hand crept slowly higher onto his pillow and he gently hugged it close, moaning slightly as in contented slumber.*' Is she awake?'* he thought.

He was lying opposed to Evette, back-to-back as was the norm now in their marital bed, waiting for a sign for continuance, or cessation of his act. The lack of further movement from her, and the return to the deepening cadence of her breath signalled the green light for the safe continuance of his need. Reaching down under his bedding, he grasped his manhood with two fingers and slowly began pulling back and forth. He was already close to coming, and instinctively he began to quicken the strokes, his breath becoming slightly harsher and shaky due to his arriving climax. He had to be careful now. *Try not to wake Evette.*

#

My eyes though were wide open now and as Adam's pace quickened, I chose the moment to pounce. Turning sharply in the bed, I grabbed the quilt, dragging the bedding away from Adam, exposing his sin fully.

"You filthy bastard!" I screamed.

For Adam, the capture proved too much. Unable to control his climax, he came all over his hand, and the bedding. I stomped over to the bedroom door, and switched on the light, leaving the naked Adam fully exposed to his humiliation.

"Jesus Christ!" he screamed, and stumbled towards the door, holding his groin to try and conceal the deed.

I stood clear as he staggered, half hunched into the bathroom at which point I took the opportunity to inspect my pristine white Egyptian Cotton sheets.

"My God! You've soiled my mother's sheets!" I screamed and began dragging the offending items from the bed.

#

In the bathroom, Adam frantically washed the sticky semen from his hand, and matted pubic hair. It was not his plan. He only wanted to have a quiet wank. A release of the pent-up sexual frustration of a man rarely called upon to perform any intimacy with his partner. If I had stayed sleeping, he could have held his climax back and enjoyed the long-lasting pleasure in his groin, before submitting to the calming release of the chemicals and hormones from his body into his brain, sending him into a deep and pleasurable sleep.

Unfortunately for him now, due to my intervention, he experienced only a frustrating mess of humiliation and shame. He shyly peered around the door at me as I stripped the bed. I could feel my face was reddened with rage. I glanced into my mirror, and saw my thin lips curled over my teeth, and brow furrowed in disgust. It was not my best look. Frantically I pulled the sheets, quilt cover and pillowcases from the bed, and stormed past Adam to the stairs.

He pleaded, "For God's sake, leave it Eve, I'll do it in the morning, it's gone midnight."

"I don't care!" I yelled as I stomped heavily down each carpeted stair, not pausing, or looking back at my pervert of a husband. "And you can sleep on the bare bed!" I added, before bursting into the kitchen switching on every light in my path.

I dragged open the washing machine door and began to stuff the bedding into the drum. I paused as I handled the bed sheet and held it aloft in the luminance of the kitchen light. Turning the sheet slowly, I found the offending wet patch left by Adam. I held the small damp circle of semen close to my nose and sniffed sharply. The smell of the pungent chlorine like semen made me gag, but worse my nose made firm contact with the liquid, and suddenly I could not get rid of the smell.

"Oh GOD!"

I gagged again and retching loudly I dropped the sheet on the grey slate kitchen floor and turned to the gleaming steel sink for refuge. Running the tap and grabbing a handful of cool water I scrubbed my nose and mouth frantically to get rid of the odour. I stood tall, while breathing deeply through my mouth, and patted her face with a soft comfort of my finest Irish Linen tea towel. Sensing cleanliness, I then braved a further inhalation through my nose, but the smell remained. I retched again and almost vomited into my sink.

I quickly hit the top of the antiseptic hand wash, squirting a blob of clear blue liquid into the palm of my hand, and then rubbed the blue soap roughly under my nose, finally obliterating any trace of Adam's foul man muck.

Adam entered, frantically trying to give me some comfort. "Are you ok Eve? I'm so sorry"

I turned away from him in disgust. I grabbed the sheet from the floor and stuffed it into the mouth of the waiting washing machine, then stooped to the kitchen sink cupboard avoiding eye contact with Adam completely. I poured a liberal dose of persil liquid into the machine, before setting the cycle to the hottest wash possible. *If the bedding was not a birthday present from my mother, I would have incinerated the lot.*

"Eve" pleaded Adam.

I turned aggressively towards him. "How could you? It's disgusting!"

He hung his head low, avoiding my harsh gaze. "I'm frustrated Eve..."

"You didn't touch me, did you?"

"God Eve, no! Well, not your breasts, only your bum. But you know how it is..."

"Oh God! Don't start that again!" I hissed and stormed past.

He stood aside submissively. "Look we should talk" he said

helplessly, knowing his efforts would be futile.

The sound of my feet stomping up the stairs was usually enough of a sign for Adam to avoid further efforts of an apology. That and my I slamming of the spare bedroom door and the scream of "Pervert!" signalled the end of the discussion.

#

Adam sighed, and walked into the hall, pausing at the foot of the stairs as he caught his reflection in the full-length designer mirror so loved by Evette. He stood sideways and studied the flatness of his stomach. Standing in his Calvin Klein boxer shorts, he made an attractive sight. Muscular, tanned, slim hips and broad shoulders, Adam could turn heads. His 'Footballers' legs that supported his pert backside were often the conversation piece of many of the women at his office, and he was the subject of some of their sexual fantasies. His thick blonde hair and light blue eyes gave him a boyish appearance, and though faithful to Evette, his childhood sweetheart, he could if he wanted, seduce many a girl with his looks alone. At 25, he was in his peak of manhood. A sexual Tyrannosaurus Rex.

If only Evette would see it.

He shrugged, and doggedly climbed the stairs to his now bare bed, and attempted to try to get through the remaining night in peace. He lay on the naked mattress, staring at the ceiling in the darkness. For a while he questioned why she was so cruel to him. '*Frigid Bitch,*' he thought, and turned angrily into his pillow, but then as soon as the thought entered his head, he dismissed the contemplation. After all, deep down he could understand her predicament. He would not want to have sex with a man himself, so why should she? And as much as his own cock gave him pleasure, he did not find it attractive, and as such if he were a woman, he would not want to touch one, let alone have it inside him or heaven forbid suck one.

But on reflection though, if he were Evette, he would at least give him some relief occasionally. Especially as she had no such reservations in giving him the odd hand job when they were courting each other at school. Almost every time they were alone, she would toss him off, catching his semen in a tissue. It kept him contented while they were engaged to be married. Not that he had much choice though, as she insisted that it was important to her that she be a virgin bride. They'd save sex for that special day.

He thought about their marriage for a moment. After nearly four years of waiting, they were married in the local church. The wedding was paid for by Evette's rich mother, left wealthy by the untimely death of Evette's father when she was a young child. Evette loved the memory of her father, though at three years old, she never really knew him. As such she was the product of his mother in laws creation, and as time progressed, Adam saw her more and more in Evette.

He did love Evette deeply though, and her happiness was paramount to him. At times like this however, he just wondered if she felt the same.

#

Unable to sleep, I laid alone in the spare room, hugging the pillow in a tense attempt to gain some comfort. Neither the bed nor the bedding was the problem. The spare or Guest Room as I liked to refer to it was in many ways furnished in more splendour and comfort than our own. My *raison d'être* is my immaculate home, and as a guest room, this was the finest of the bedrooms. Perfection in *Feng Shui* but with all my girlie touches, just as I like it. It was also my private dressing room, away from the prying eyes of Adam, and as such, it is my haven of comfort. It was my anger and frustration at Adam that was causing my temporary insomnia.

We have argued many times over sex. Always caused by Adam's insistence that it was the natural thing for a loving couple to do of course.

Why couldn't he just accept the fact that I do not want to do it anymore? It's not that we are 'Newly Weds,' We have been married for five years now, and I has never been any different. Why does he feel the need to have sex anyway? We have sex every month as it is, now that we are trying for a child.

He should be grateful.

Many of my friends are the same as me, and I am certain their husbands would not resort to playing with themselves in their bed, while their wives slept.

It's disgusting!

I shuddered at the thought.

Adam must be abnormal. Maybe he should visit our G.P? He needs medical help. And quick!

Happy that I had probably found a path to a potential cure for Adam's perversion, I fell into a contented slumber.

2

BABY STEPS

The following morning Adam tentatively knocked on the door of the Guest room. He had prepared my usual breakfast of two slices of lightly buttered toast and marmalade, and a cup of cappuccino, which were balanced carefully on the Villeroy & Boch natural wood tea tray.

I did not respond to his gentle knock. Although I was awake, I was still seething after the previous night's fiasco, and I wanted Adam to know just exactly how angry I was. He slowly opened the door to see my back turned away from him. I moved slightly to signify that I was awake but was not in the mood to fully show it.

"Eve, are you awake? I've made you some breakfast"

"Just put it down Adam, I'm not really in the mood now." I replied wearily.

He hesitated. The act of placing a tray down amongst the numerous "Cherished Teddy" figures adorning one dresser unit and all of my perfume bottles, face creams and make up accessories on the other, was not an easy task. He stood still.

"Put it where Eve?"

"God Adam, you love to make things awkward, don't you?" I reluctantly moved over to the far side of the mattress but declined to look at him. He placed the tray on the bed.

"Are you still upset Eve?"

"Yes Adam! I cannot understand why you feel the need to do that filthy thing while I'm sleeping. You could have gone in the toilet."

He sighed at the realisation that another pointless argument over our sex life was about to unfold.

"I didn't want to disturb you, and if I got up to the toilet, you would have asked what I was doing, and then we would have argued again!"

I turned and faced him, scowling.

"Yes! I would because I cannot understand why you are so sex obsessed! It was bad enough I caught you tossing off to that Sky channel when you were supposed to be watching football"

"Here we go..." said Adam, under his breath.

"Porn Adam. Porn! You brought Porn into our house, and now you are assaulting me in my bed, while you play with yourself. Where is it going to end Adam? Rape?"

He took a deep breath. I could see his mind whirring as he carefully chose his reply so not to exacerbate the situation.

"I am normal Eve, all men masturbate"'

"Do they? Not every day like you Adam. None of my friend's partners do"

"Oh, so you discuss our marital problems with them. Thanks, Eve, I bet they think I am a right wanker"

"I don't mention you by name, I just say someone I know"

"Oh, that's ok then, there's no fucking way they'd think you were talking about us!" he said sarcastically. He scowled as his temper rose within.

"If you wasn't such a frigid cow, I wouldn't have to wank! So, before you judge me Eve, look at your fucking self."

I did not answer, but turned back into my pillow, facing away from him. Adam tutted loudly, then grabbing the tray and withdrawing his peace offering, he turned to walk out.

"I'm going to work"

"Well make sure you are home early, as I'm booking you an appointment to see Katrina for tonight"

Adam halted at the door. He only knew of one Katrina, our General Practitioner, and long-term friend of my mother.

"Your doctor friend? No – Fucking- Way Eve"

"You need help Adam. You're going!"

Adam stood looking at me, waiting for me to at least turn around, but I had gone into sulk mode.

"Eve... Everybody masturbates. I do, your dad probably did"

That got my attention! I turned angrily at Adam's audacity to mention my dad in such a context.

"Don't say that Adam. Don't you dare talk about him in that way."

"Eve, he did..."

I grabbed the another pillow and pushed one into each ear to block out the spurious allegation.

" .. in fact, I bet he wanked himself into a stupor everyday rather than shag your frosty old bat of a mother!"

Despite the pillows, I still heard Adam's taunt but chose to ignore them. He stood in a brief silence, contemplating his next move. I know that he hated rowing and made a point of trying never to depart during cross words, so he decided to try and reconcile the situation before going to work.

"Eve, babe...."

"Don't call me that"

"What? Babe?"

I sat and turned frostily to Adam, pulling the quilt high to hide any view of her body from my depraved husband.

"Yes! I am not a pig, nor some Essex girl."

"I know", he paused and then smiled, "But we do live in Harlow"

I took the bait.

"Church Langley Adam" I retorted, referring to the middle-class housing estate in Essex that was our home. I hate the fact that we have to live in Essex. Even though I was born there. The growing trend of the "Essex Babe", and the infamous TOWIE show had made my county cheap.

Determined to prove my point, I leapt from the bed and marched into our bedroom. Dragging open the wardrobe door, I grabbed a handful of my designer shoes, shaking them at Adam, who had followed sheepishly behind with tray in hand.

"Look! Louie Vuitton! Prada! Jimmy Choo! Can you see any white high heels here?"

He smiled and pointed to the white high heel diamante shoes tucked surreptitiously to the rear of the wardrobe. I stared poker faced at him from my crouched position in front of the door.

"They're Iridescent! Not White Adam!" I said, correcting him.

From his lofty viewpoint Adam found himself staring down the front of Evette's Burberry camisole at my bare breasts. He smiled, and instinctively raised his eyebrows.

I noticed the slight offline of Adam's gaze and knew where his eyes dwelled. I snatched at the front of my top and stood abruptly turning away from him and groped in the wardrobe for my dressing gown. But, in my haste to wrangle it from the hanger, I dropped it to the floor and had to stoop to retrieve it. Being a former gymnast at school, I am very flexible, and bent over without the slightest bend of my knees. As my Camisole lifted Adam, now was able to admire my small yet rounded bottom, and as my legs parted slightly, I inadvertently bared all.

Adam stared longingly at me, and instantly aroused his erection grew quickly. He loved my body. My large firm breasts, and perfect round nipples, long legs, flat stomach, but with just the right amount of weight to cover her slender frame. I would almost always refer to my body as fat, but Adam preferred "Voluptuous", and it was obvious to me that he adored every curve.

I closed the wardrobe, pausing to look into the full-length mirrored door and into the eyes of Adam standing behind me. Placing the tray onto the dressing table, he swiftly approached, and placed his arms firmly around my waist. I tried to pull away, but he held her firm. He kissed my ear, then my neck from the tip of her ear to the shoulder, in a swift passionate embrace. I grabbed his hands but I protested weakly.

"No Adam, I can't do this..."

"Yes, you can" he whispered, his breathing growing rapid with excitement. He glided his hands over the silk Camisole top, cupping my breasts from below. Lifting them slightly, he circled his fingers over my nipples bringing them to a firm erection, and then pinched them softly between his ring and middle fingers. He gently pushed his erection into the softness of my bottom, and ran his hand slowly down my stomach. Caressing me gently across the top of my pubic mound, he slowly yet firmly began to masturbate me.

I was completely taken by surprise, and the forceful yet gentleness of Adam was a complete turn on. I felt myself losing control, and in my mind I had to try and regain dominance of the situation. *This was not how it should be... What am I doing?*

"Adam... Adam...... Adam.. STOP!"

"What? What's wrong?"

"You know I can't do it just like that. It's not right"

He sighed heavily and turned away frustrated. He released me from his grasp, and I ran into the bathroom. *I was not finished though. This had to be done right.*

“Just stay there Adam” I ordered, to which he sat on the bed, staring at his reflection in the mirror.

Adam raised his hands slightly in disbelief and mouthed “What the Fuck?” to his opposite image. Irritated he breathed steadily to control his anger.

In the bathroom I quickly rummaged around the vanity unit for my special sex equipment, leaving Adam to stew on the bed.

I returned to the bedroom, holding a digital thermometer in my mouth, and sat on the bed next to Adam, not speaking for half a minute until the reading was complete.

“I should have done this before I got out of bed” I said indifferently.

Adam stared at his reflection in the mirror. He knew what was occurring. It was time for his monthly mating session.

“Why are you doing this? We could have just made love naturally Eve.”

Ignoring him, I opened the dresser drawer, and removed my Basal Body temperature Fertility guide chart, and studied it and the thermometer intently. Satisfied, I threw the chart and thermometer into the drawer, and slid back onto the bed. I quickly pulled two pillows from under the quilt, shoved them under my hips, and pulled my Camisole up above her waist. I smiled at Adam.

“Come on then Adam, stick it in”

I could see Adam’s passion was all but killed by that moment of my clinical sexual surrender. As much as he wanted to make love, the thought of having to mate in order to impregnate her made it extremely hard to gain his now flagging erection. Ever the obliging husband though, he turned to me, and tried to regain his sexual desire. He climbed onto the bed, and gently lay between my thighs. He slowly kissed my neck, and began to slide his hand under my top, lifting it to expose my breasts. I grabbed his hand and pulled it from under her Camisole. But my mind was now on other more important things the sex.

“I don’t want all that,” I said coldly. Adam looked at me briefly.

“Why not?”

“We don’t have time Adam; you have to go to work...”

“Not for an hour Eve!” he protested.

“It’s not all about you Adam, I have to do the washing, then there’s the ironing, and I’ve got to meet Melisa for lunch.”

Adam angrily pushed himself up onto his knees.

"Oh God! Shall I just fuck you now then Eve? Or shall I wank in a test tube, and you can squirt it up your fanny later?"

"Oh, for God's sake Adam, don't be so crude"

I scorned at him briefly, then with a roll of my eyes I pulled her Camisole up slightly then grabbing Adam's left hand I pushed it under my top, and onto my breast.

"Get on with it please!"

Adam sighed, he pulled his hand free, removed his boxer shorts, and again lay between my thighs. He moved into position, but the moment of passion was almost gone. His erection failing, he could not manage penetration. Pushing hard, his cock simply bent against me. *This is useless..* It was not helped by my drying up, but I was resilient.

"What's the matter Adam?"

"Isn't it bloody obvious Eve? This isn't really doing it for me is it? You'll have to help me in"

"Oh God Adam!" I hissed.

I reluctantly reached down between Adam's legs, but when I felt the half erect penis, I couldn't help but withdraw my hand abruptly. His cock was limp, cold and slightly wet like a raw sausage. *Yuck!* I wiped my hand on the sheets to cleanse my palm.

"Ugh! No! I can't touch it Adam, you'll have to play with it."

"For fuck sake!" he moaned and lifting his hips he attempted to rub his failing erection into action. The tension of the moment though was proving too great, and even his own cock was beginning to desert him. Frustrated he began to lift my top and expose my breasts to give him some visual stimulation. I wasn't having that! I resisted and pulled it down.

"You're not looking at me while you're doing that!" I barked.

"You know what? Fuck it! I'm going to work."

Adam stood from the bed and began putting on his boxer shorts, hopping around on one leg in his haste to dress. I suddenly realised that the moment of maximum fertility may be passing, I quickly pleaded with Adam.

"I'm sorry, I'm sorry Adam. I'll let you look at me, I'm sorry."

I hated this situation, but reluctantly I removed my top, and my large round breasts fell into view. I had to act *sexy* to get him interested again, so knelt on the bed and pushed my breasts forward seductively and whispered.

"Come on Adam, suck my nipples."

I lifted my left breast, and rose high on my knees, while placing my other hand around Adam's neck as he stood helpless, one half leg in his shorts, and balancing on the other. I pulled his face into the soft flesh of my breast, and he sucked slowly and eagerly on my nipple. I then pulled him on top of the bed, and he lay between my legs, sucking one breast then the other. My nipples when erect, were particularly sensitive, and I could feel myself succumbing to Adam's need.

But we need to get on with it!

Although I found myself enjoying his attention to my breasts, there was a more pressing task for him to fill. I reached down and grabbed Adam's now rock-hard shaft, pulling him into me, and he quickly began to thrust gently in and out. He kissed my neck and began to kiss around my mouth. I didn't want all this. I pulled away.

"No, just do it, come up now."

Adam stared at me, "You're joking right?"

I forced a half-hearted smile across my face. Unbeknown to me, it reminded Adam of the day he met my mother, and the overly polite yet cold smile she had greeted him with that day, barely able to hide the disappointment on her face. I had to get him back in the game, and so I rubbed his back roughly, kind of how most people would pat a dog. But it wasn't really doing it for him.

"You're in now Adam," I said, "just hurry up and come now, we've got to get on."

To Adam, I had sounded like his *own* mother trying to encourage him to go to the dentist. His dick almost fell into slumber.

"I can't do this, sorry." He climbed off of me once more.

"No no Adam, look, just toss yourself off, I'll stay still, and you can watch me. Once you start coming shove it in."

"I'm not doing that."

"You did it easy enough when I was asleep Adam," I said scathingly.

My words could not have been more off putting. He was now angry but sexually frustrated, so he obliged.. He knelt between my legs as I raised them high and I closed my eyes tight. I grabbed both my breasts in each hand and comically held them together as if offering them to a herd of hungry babies, aiming to squirt milk into the mouths of each one. I lay with my legs open wide, exposing myself completely, and surrendered. I just wanted this over.

#

Adam grabbed his half erect member, and with the other hand took hold of Evette's breast. She dropped her hands to each side in surrender as Adam began to masturbate furiously, the tip of his cock rubbing against the lips of her vagina. Ignoring the distain on her face during the act, his concentration on her round breasts soon brought him to climax within a minute. As he came, he pushed deep into Evette, and with a few final thrusts the deed was done.

Adam though partially satisfied, felt cheap. He rose from the bed and turned to go to the bathroom and shower. Evette though had one more request.

#

He finally finished, *Thank God.* But he had one more important task to do.

"Hang on Adam, you need to raise my legs." I said,

I held both my legs elevated in a perfect "V", and shoved a pillow under my hips.

"What?"

"You have to grab my legs and hold me up."

Adam stood; hands raised slightly in mild bewilderment.

"Why do I have to do that?"

"So, your semen can swim downwards of course. It's easier for them."

He turned, and slowly climbed onto the bed and stood above me. Pulling both legs high he heaved me upwards, so my hips were completely raised from the bed.

"We have to wait two minutes now," I said, my voice strangulated by the ridiculous pose. I closed my eyes, imagining as his baby makers swimming down , racing towards my waiting love egg.

#

Adam looked down at her. Both her breasts had fallen into her arm pits like two large water wings. Her head was contorted giving her a chinless appearance, and her eyes though shut, were bulging due to the slight asphyxiation. She reminded him of Gonzo from the Muppet show. To crown it all, he had the dubious privilege of staring down her gaping vagina.

I am never, ever going to do this again... he thought.

3

HE … WAGGLES

I sat in the small waiting room at the General Practitioners surgery. I had phoned my G.P personally asking for an emergency appointment and was the last remaining patient. Irritably I waited, seeking solace from face Book on my iPhone. My attention was interrupted mid "face-booking" my closest friend Melisa by the Dr's receptionist, who seemed slightly peeved at my presence.

"Ms Barker-McCardle? Dr Bailey will see you now."

I gathered myself, throwing my iPhone into my white leather Louie Vuitton *Suhall Le Talenteux* shoulder bag, and marched purposefully to Dr Bailey's examination room. I had been going over this meeting in my mind, and I was more than a little nervous about discussing our sex lives with the Katrina, but I had to do something. Now! I took a deep breath, and prepared for my performance. Not bothering to knock, I opened the door with vigour, stepped in and all but collapsed into the patient's seat.

Dr Katrina Bailey is a large overweight forty something woman, with a no-nonsense attitude to her profession. She looked up at me as I entered, and appeared surprised at my sudden intrusion. Wearing her usual miss-matched fashion disaster regalia, she was not *de rigour* of my mother's friends. But if you wanted an honest and frank opinion, Dr Katrina Bailey was the person that all of my family came to.

"Oh God, do come in Evette! Make yourself at home," she said in a slightly startled manner.

I ran my hand through my hair, to emphasise the magnitude of the problem that I was about to unload on Dr Bailey.

"Sorry Katrina, but I had to see you urgently." I said, and then I unexpectedly burst into tears. *OMG, This really is serious!*

Katrina was suddenly concerned.

"Oh child, what's wrong?" She stood and placed an arm around me.

"It's not me, it's Adam," I sobbed, "he's been .... well horrible. I don't think I can take much more."

"There now, I'm sure it can't be all that bad. Is Adam here with you?"

"No, he refused to come and see you."

"Why? I don't quite understand. Is it you or Adam who is ill?"

I sniffed and dabbed my eyes with the back of my hand. *The emotion was real! I really am stressed!*

"Neither, well not physically anyway. I think he has some mental issues, and he won't get any help. I don't know what to do."

Katrina could tell a drama was about to unfold. She rang the receptionist, and told her to go and briefly departed the room to make us a cup of coffee.

I sat in the surgery and took the opportunity to begin a feverish exchange of texts with Melisa, to share the crisis in my head. Katrina then returned with two mugs of coffee.

"Right, put that bloody phone away Evette, and tell me what the problem is. I take it that the problem is you and Adam?"

"I don't know if I can tell you." I said. As a distraction, more than a need, I began to drink from the coffee cup, but the sight of the stained porcelain and a slight crack halted me in my tracks. *Gross* .. I placed the cup down and to avoid drinking the brew, and to be honest, I feigned a further tear shedding session. Accepting a tissue from Katrina, I steadied myself to explain the troubles with Adam. I blew my nose loudly into the tissue, then handed it back to Katrina Bailey, who rather scornfully took it from me at fingertips before dropping it into the bin. Standing to wash her hands, she turned, shaking water droplets in my general direction with a subtle hint of retribution.

"Well Evette, I think you need to tell me what's wrong, or I cannot possibly help you."

"It's our sex life!" I blurted shamefully.

"It often is," said Katrina, "what exactly is it though? Are you not getting on sexually?"

"Well, I think so. We are trying for a baby, but it's never enough for him. He always wants more, and now...."

Katrina leant forward showing interest. "Now?"

"He just ... I can't say it. This is so embarrassing."

"It's ok Evette, I have heard it all before. Just tell me."

"It's Adam, he is doing perverted things to me."

Katrina looked slightly shocked but tried not to show any change of emotion. She had met Adam once or twice and thought he was the perfect young man.

"What exactly is he doing Evette? "

"I can't say." I could feel my eyes filling with tears. Katrina again put a comforting arm around me. She felt protective over me, as if she could see the child she once knew, and held a soft spot for. I found myself enjoying the attention and I literally sobbed for England.

"Just tell me. If it is that bad, we can go to the Police if you like. They can protect you from Adam. You do not have to take that sort of abuse Evette."

The Police?. I had not thought of the possible consequence of embellishing our relationship problems to Katrina, so I decided to get on with the story.

"Oh no, please no. It's not that bad really."

"But Evette, what is it dear? You are so upset."

I took a deep breath. Although I was certain Adam was annoyingly over sexed, and a bit perverted, I did often wonder if I was making too much of our problems. Now was the time to find out.

"He… waggles…" I said, looking deeply ashamed. Katrina looked both confused and slightly amused.

"Waggles? What on earth is a waggle?"

"Waggling, well that's what I think it's called," said Evette. The look of confusion and wry smile on Katrina's face, prompted a more explicit demonstration, so I made a circular shape with my thumb and forefinger, then swiftly moved my hand up and down an imaginary penis in my lap. Katrina laughed out loud.

"Waggling! You mean wanking!" she chuckled.

"I don't like to use that term Katrina, it's revolting!" I replied tersely.

"I'm sorry Evette, but how long have you been married?"

"Five years, so there is no need for him to do that is there?"

"I don't know Evette, but in my experience, it is perfectly natural for men to do it."

"But he did it in our bed" I protested.

Katrina shook her head, with an amused expression on her face.

She thinks this is a bloody joke!

I could see that Katrina was about to side with Adam, so I offered further damming substantiation of Adam's perversion. "And I caught him watching pornography! Surely that's wrong?"

Katrina's expression said it all. She wasn't alarmed or distressed as I was expecting.

"Men do watch porn, as do many women. Why should you be so worried, does he make you watch or something?"

"No, but I caught him downstairs waggling over a Sky program with naked women on the phone."

Katrina chuckled, "Evette, he is a young man. Maybe you should both try and improve your sex lives."

"No!" I replied bluntly. "He is getting plenty. We are trying for children, so every month when I am ovulating, we try. Only last night, I woke to find him waggling in bed. And he admitted touching me when I was sleeping!"

Katrina chuckled again.

I was more than a little peeved now.

"Katrina! You're not taking this seriously at all. Are you?"

"Please darling. I'm not sure you really have that much of a problem Evette."

Frustrated at being treated lightly by Dr Bailey caused my anger to rise.

"Well listen to this if you think that he is normal." I said crossly.

"This morning he did it over Virginia." I sat with arms crossed tightly over my chest and sat staring haughtily at Katrina.

"I'm sorry? What? He did what over who?"

"Adam squirted.... over Virginia. I was nearly sick."

Katrina was dumb founded. "I'm sorry dear, squirted what? And who is Virginia?"

Oh my God, she is going to make me say it.. I raised my hands above my waist, then motioned both hands at my own crutch.

"He squirted his semen into my Virginia. Is that plain enough for you Katrina?"

Katrina could not contain her laughter, and guffawed loudly, snorting and giggling. Her whole body jiggled with her mirth, causing me to squirm uncomfortably.

"I'm sorry, you mean vagina I assume?" giggled Katrina, without a single futile attempt to subdue her amusement.

"Yes, but I hate that word Katrina. It's so gross!"

"I'm sorry love, but that is what a vagina is called."

After a series of guffaws and un-lady like snorts, Katrina finally regained some composure and returned to her professional persona.

"But anyway, I take it you were asleep, and he masturbated over your... Virginia. I must agree, that is a little weird."

"Oh no, I wasn't sleeping. We were having sex, but he could not do it, as I put him off apparently, even though I did take my top off for him. But I wanted his semen in me to get pregnant, so I shut my eyes and told him to squirt it in."

I could tell my scenario depicted had swayed Katrina's sympathy towards Adam.

Poor Bugger... she is probably thinking! Thanks Katrina!

"Look, I think that maybe you and he could do with some counselling. I will put you in touch with a colleague of mine who specialises in matrimonial problems. But from what you have told me, Adam is probably no different than any other man, and perhaps you should both seek help with your relationship."

Although I was not completely satisfied, I agreed. Maybe another professional who did not know Adam or I might be the answer. I politely thanked Katrina and departed feeling slightly guilty at bothering her with our problems.

I slumped back to my car to gather my thoughts. A Facebook status may bring an answer, so I wrote to my many friends.

'Mood really low now, must do much soul searching. Why do men never realise just how much they can hurt a girl.'

There was the usual flurry of '*what's wrong Hun?*' and likes, but no one really seemed to be interested. However, there was always one more person I could confide in and always rely on before making a decision.

Melisa would know what to do.

4

MELISA TO THE RESCUE

Melisa arrived in dramatic fashion, screeching to a halt on the drive of our house in her bright pink Nissan Figaro Coupe.

Tuesday being Adam's Gym night, I had taken the opportunity to invite Melisa, my lifelong friend and confidant, to our home. We have been friends since nursery school and shared most things and experiences together. Following my non-productive session with Katrina Bailey, I needed further support in my disastrous sexual problems with Adam. I stood at the door, hanky in hand as Melisa jumped from the car.

"Oh my God Evette! What's happened?"

I did not reply but turned and marched into the living room and slumped onto my sofa, hanky held under my nose. Melisa quickly removed her shoes and followed, climbing onto the sofa next to me, hugging me close as I began to sob.

"What's wrong Hun? Please tell me?"

I must confess, these were 'crocodile tears' coming from me, but I needed Melisa's absolute attention, and this was the best way to get it. I steadied my emotions then told the whole sorry story, but as I did, I began to notice a change in Melisa's body language.

"You don't seem that bothered Mel?" I sniffed. Then it became apparent that Melisa could not hide her amusement further.

"I'm sorry" she chuckled. "I thought he had hurt you, not that he had a crafty wank!"

"He *has* hurt me! It's not normal!"

I began to cry again uncontrollably, but real tears this time.

Everyone is turning against me..

Melisa had seen me cry like this before and although she often said that I was a bit of a drama queen, she usually responded to my needs. Plus, she loved a bit of juicy gossip, and was not going to miss out, so she gave me her full attention.

"I know just the thing," she said, and then left the room and darted into the kitchen where the wine rack lay. Selecting a bottle of *Chateauneuf du Pape* and two crystal wine glasses, she filled them to the brim before returning.

"Here, drink!" she ordered. I duly obliged.

"Look Evette, I really do not think you have a problem with Adam. For one he worships you, secondly, he is normal, and men do like a wank!"

"Don't say that, I hate that word"

"Okay, he masturbates! And last but no means least, he is totally fucking hot! So, you should be happy!"

"Happy?" I said incredulously. "How can I be happy living with a sexual deviant?"

"Okay, I'll have him"

"What? You think it's normal?"

Melisa laughed "Yeah! I'd watch him. Then I'd totally fuck him!"

"Mel!"

"What do you expect? Evette he is gorgeous! And to be fair if you don't fancy him maybe you should get some help. Or let me have a go"

"I do fancy him. But when it comes to sex, I just can't do it." I sighed. I drank down the contents of my wineglass. Melisa quickly refilled my drink.

"Maybe you're really gay Evette?"

I scowled at the accusation. "I most certainly am not Mel!"

"Well... I remember a girl who once …"

"Don't mention that!" I snapped.

"Eve, you remember."

"No, I was drunk and ... No "

Melisa laughed teasingly, "I remember… Mel and Evette sitting in a tree K.I.S.S.I.N.G ! Ha Ha! you remember!"

"I don't! it was a long time ago Mel and I don't remember it like that"

"And you touched my fanny Eve!" giggled Melisa.

I suddenly became angry, "no Melisa! Stop it, this is serious."

Melisa sighed, as her giggles faded. She cleared her throat to gain composure and return to the serious subject of Adam's and my relationship.

"Okay, sorry. I shan't mention it again."

"Thank you"

"Perhaps Evette you need some professional help"

"That's what Katrina said. She started to tell me about someone, but I can't remember who it was."

"Did she give you a number or something?"

"I don't think she did"

Evette was feeling lost and again sighed, the emotion was almost too much to bear. She sought comfort in her rapidly emptying glass once more.

"Steady" said Melisa. "I'll have to open another bottle soon."

"There's another in the rack" I sniffed, draining the glass once more.

Melisa left the room briefly to grab another bottle, whilst I searched my bag for a clean tissue to wipe my eyes. As I pulled a tissue from my bag, a brightly coloured business card fell to the floor. I picked it up and studied the print. The card had a hologram image on the centre of a blue woman, clothed in ornate Indian dress. Underneath were the words "Rati, the Hindu Goddess of Love".

As I moved the card, the four slender arms of the Goddess moved slowly and gracefully up and down, and her eyes seemed to penetrate my gaze. The card colours changed and flashed from blue to gold brightly and hypnotically, as I stared into the eyes of the deity.

"What's that?" interrupted Mel, returning with another bottle of red. She grabbed the card from my hand.

"It must have come from Katrina," I said.

Glancing at the picture on the front briefly, Melisa turned the card over and read it aloud.

"Dr Kumaran Saha .... Sahasra ... budhhe ."

"What?"

"This is what the card says, Dr Kumaran Sahasra ... Sahasrabudhhe "

Melisa showed the back of the card as she handed it back to me.

'Dr Kumaran Sahasrabudhhe, BPsy (Hons) MA, BACP. M.D MRC Pysch.

Psychosexual therapist, Relationship Counsellor .

The Rivers Hospital Sawbridgeworth.'

"It's only local Evette, give him a call"

I stared at the card for a few more seconds but tossed it back in my bag.

"I can't see that I need too. Adam should go."

"But he won't go, will he?"

"No"

"So, it's up to you Eve, it's the only way."

"But what if he's rubbish? What if he's some fake or something?"

Melisa laughed. "What? Like some perverted fat old Indian bloke with a big moustache? Recording your inner most secrets, and sexual fantasies! And WANKING over it" she giggled loudly. I shuddered at the thought.

"Maybe you're right, he might be fake. I shouldn't bother"

"I was joking! Look, he's at The Rivers! He's got to be decent. You need help!"

"I know .." I said glumly. I sought comfort in my glass, and stared at the TV on the wall, even though it was switched off. Melisa though, eager to lighten the mood, had a brainwave.

"I know. If Dr Ta-Ra-Ra Boom-De-Ay or whatever his name is can't help. Bridget Jones can!" and grabbing the remote control, she quickly found *Bridget Jones Diary* on the TV. Melisa then cuddled up to me on the sofa, and with glasses in hand we sought solace in a chick flick.

The mysterious card however kept playing on my mind.

5

DOCTOR SAHASRABUDHHE

The Rivers private Hospital in Harlow was well known by reputation as a professional and high-class establishment. I had called the number on the card and made an appointment for a consultation on the automated answerphone system, taking the first steps to cure our failing marriage. Adam had no idea what was going on, and was at work, so with Melisa as my 'wing man' and chauffeur, we arrived at the busy car park in the rural settings of the hospital.

"Fuck it's busy here" said Melisa, after driving around several times to find somewhere to park. She stopped the Figaro next to a series of Porta Cabins which were erected around some building work occurring in the grounds.

"Look, stay here and I'll go into the reception Evette and ask where we are supposed to park. I don't want to get clamped or get a fine. If someone comes tell them that I'll be back in a minute. Can I take his card? I'll never be able to pronounce his name"

I handed the card to Melisa and she got out and walked towards the main building. I waited nervously. I was certain in my mind that we needed professional help but I was unsure if I should be there without having consulted Adam or having him with me. I turned on the radio. A soft chilled out tune was playing, and I closed my eyes briefly to relax. The sun was shining and warm against my face through the window, and I found myself drifting off to sleep.

A gentle knocking on the glass woke me. I looked up to see a figure standing next to the passenger door. I wound down the window and looked into a handsome dark smiling face of a tall Indian man. He had chiselled cheekbones, and strong chin which was covered by a short and groomed beard. He had long thick black hair tied back against his head. His eyes were deep brown and warm, and his smile showed beautifully white teeth. He wore a long beige coloured Sherwani coat, embroidered with gold, and looked as if he was about to attend an Indian wedding or celebration.

"Hello" he said softly. "By any chance are you looking for Dr Sahasrabudhhe?"

"Yes! How did you know?"

"I am magic of course. You must be Ms Barker-McCardle?"

I nodded, smiling at this handsome man before me.

"Please, follow me" he said, and gestured with both hands for me to leave the car.

I hesitated, "I am waiting for my friend, she'll be back in a minute."

"She will know where to come. Please, the clock is ticking. I charge by the hour remember?"

He laughed gently, then opened the car door and guided me out, taking my hand gracefully. We walked to the nearest builders cabin in the compound area, and he opened the door.

I suddenly became concerned. *'Surely, he would not have an office here! In a yard!'* I hesitated at the door.

"It's okay," he said warmly. "It is a temporary arrangement, follow me through the other door and you will see."

On the far side of the cabin was a second door, through which I followed him, and we were once again outside but in a beautiful ornate walled garden. The walls were covered in Orange Blossom shrubs and Jasmine, giving off a wonderful fragrance as we entered. A central walkway crossed a wide symmetrical two-tiered pool, with a continual waterfall trickling down gently rocking the lotus flowers floating majestically on the surface. The sound of falling water and the wonderful scents from the flowers filled the space with relaxing ambience.

On the far end of the walkway was a large hanging wicker chair-swing, adorned with gold ornate cushions. Next to this was a matching lounger, with a small oak table between them with two long glasses and a small brass incense lamp.

"Please, make yourself comfortable." He indicated to the lounger; I cautiously sat on the edge.

"Here, try this" he said, handing me a clear long glass of red liquid chilled with ice. I accepted the drink without question, looking admiringly at the beautiful garden settings and taking in the aromatic ambience.

"It is Iced Rose tea. It will help you relax."

"I am fine, thanks. It is so beautiful here, not what I expected when we walked through the building."

"A calm mind brings inner strength and self-confidence, so that's very important for good health. The Dalai Lama said that. You are a little apprehensive I feel. Lie back in the lounger, then when you are ready tell me your problems. I assume that you have some?" he chuckled.

I laid back into the comfortable lounger, placing the drink onto the table. There was something enchantingly relaxing in the garden that almost made me forget why I was there. Part of my attention though was on the handsome dark-skinned prince sat beside me. I found myself smiling serenely at him, gazing into his eyes like a bewitched teenager at a pop concert. I quickly steadied my mind and pushed my issues with Adam to the forefront.

"It's my husband Adam, he is... well, over demanding."

"In what way?"

"In an intimate way."

"Tell me more, how demanding?"

"He wants it all the time basically."

"And? How often does he get it? daily? Once? Twice? More?"

I shook my head between each question. "Does that matter? I don't see how often he gets it matters?"

"If you say he is too demanding it may. Do you make love daily?"

"No."

"Weekly?"

"NO! what bloody difference does that make? He does get it, but he wants it all the time. It's not natural."

"I have to disagree; it is perfectly natural."

My temper began to rise. *Another bloody person who thinks it's me!*

"Okay, is it natural then for him to masturbate while I am in bed. Sleeping by the way!"

"No and yes. If you are not happy then no. If you are, then yes."

"I'm not. I don't understand why he needs sex so much. I don't understand why he wants to see me naked. I don't understand why he must masturbate or look at porn. I don't understand any of it. I don't understand him at all."

"Would it help if you could. If you were able to see things from his own eyes for instance?"

"I don't see how I can. It's hopeless."

"I think that it would help if you could see things from Adam's perspective."

"What about him seeing *my* perspective?"

"He is not here; I can only work with you. I promise that after today you will maybe understand what it is like to be him. After all, this is all about understanding Adam, yes?"

I nodded and laid back into the comfort of the cushions.

"I think it may help if I ask you some basic relationship questions. Just say the first thing that comes into your head. Be honest with yourself"

He handed me the iced tea, then lit the incense lamp on the table.

"It is Nag Champa, it too will help you relax. Do you like Tantra music?"

I took a nervous sip of the red tea, "I don't know."

"You will love it. It is very sensual"

He reached over and placed his hands around mine, guiding the glass to my lips.

"Now Drink it all, you are hot, no?"

Strangely, I did feel suddenly warm and finished the drink quickly. He gently touched my shoulders then laid me back into the soft cushions. As he spoke, I felt suddenly relaxed, surrendering to the calm voice of the Doctor.

The fragrant smells from the incense and the surrounding garden wafted over me. I closed my eyes as the sounds of a sitar rang out, accompanied by a rhythmic drumming, and flute.

"Imagine that you and Adam are alone. Adam is looking at your body, what do you feel?"

"Uncomfortable."

"Why?"

"I don't like him looking at me."

"In what way, imagine that he is looking at you right now, what is he looking at that makes you uncomfortable?"

"At my breasts. He is always staring at them, trying to look down my top."

Suddenly, the Doctors voice was directly in my left ear, whispering softly. "They *are* magnificent, you do have beautiful breasts though."

I shot open my eyes and lifted my head looking sharply to the left, then right expecting to find Dr Sahasrabudhhe right next to my ear, but he was sitting in his seat cross legged looking at me.

"Are you okay?" he said.

I was confused. "Sorry, I thought you whispered in my ear"

He laughed softly. "No, what did I say?"

"It was nothing, I think I must have imagined it"

"Now relax, listen to my voice but try not to open your eyes. I need to know that you are completely relaxed through this procedure."

I laid back once more.

"Adam is naked, standing in front of you. How do you feel?"

"Angry."

"Why? What is he doing?"

"Nothing, he is just standing there. But I can see his penis."

"Is it big?"

"What?"

"Is he aroused?"

I could see Adam clearly now. Muscular, naked, aroused. The music seemed to quicken and grow in intensity. My image of Adam now seemed darker in colour, his hair long and black, his eyes brown, he looked remarkably like.. *the Doctor.*

Dr Sahasrabudhhe whispered again in my ear, "What is he doing? What is he saying?"

What the fuck?

I then physically felt him lift me gently upright and felt him slide onto the lounger behind me. I could not move, I felt helpless, but my eyes remained shut as I felt his breath on my neck.

"You are beautiful" he whispered. "Is he behind you? Touching you? Caressing your breasts?"

His hands glided under my arms, cupping my breasts. He tenderly kissed my neck and ear lobes. My clothes seemed to fall easily from my body, and in no time I was completely naked, enjoying every passionate kiss from my neck to my breasts and nipples. I could not resist, as all of my usual inhibitions had melted away in the caress of the Doctor and the ambience of sensual sounds and smells.

My eyes still closed in ecstasy, I felt him move from behind me, and he gently pushed my legs wide, lifting them over his own thighs. Softly kissing my mouth, he pulled me close as he entered me and then slowly began to move back and forth, lifting me as he pushed deeply. I gasped and threw my arms around his neck; I passionately kissed his neck and shoulders. The music seemed to rise as I quickly began to reach my climax. The drumming also grew louder, faster, and more intense as the Doctor thrust deeper and harder into me.

Bang Bang, Bang Bang, BANG BANG ! BANG BANG! BANG BANG BANG BANG!

"What the fuck Evette?" came a familiar angry cry from somewhere, "Open the fucking door!"

Melisa's shouts and the banging on the Figaro window brought me sharply into the real world. I looked quickly to my left and saw Melisa's face pressed against the glass of the window. Then, much to my horror I realised that I was sitting with my knickers pulled down to my thighs, and my hand was almost buried into my crutch! I whipped my hand out, and hurriedly pulled my knickers up fully.

I unlocked the door and Melisa almost threw it back from the hinge. "Jesus Fucking Christ Eve! You were masturbating in a public car park! What the fucking fuck?"

"I wasn't! I was ... What? Oh My God! I was! What is going on?"

Melisa shut the door with a bang, then rushed around to the driver's door, and dived into the car. She laughed nervously "Christ Eve, I thought you were here to see Doctor What's his name to sort your sex life out. Not take matters into your own hands!"

"I don't understand," I said confused, "I saw him."

"Where? Did you speak to him, as the reception have never heard of him"?

"No, He came to the car, and took me into a garden, then we had a consultation, then he gave me a drink, and …"

"You couldn't have done; I've only been five minutes Eve!"

Melisa's words hit hard; *she must be wrong*.

"No, no no no ... something's wrong here. I was in there, in a garden, I spoke to him, then we… we ...He drugged me, he must have drugged me."

"What? What Eve? I've literally been five minutes if that!"

"What? That can't be.. I.. something's wrong here. I'm going to see him!"

I threw open the door of the Figaro and climbed out of the car hurriedly. I marched over to the Builders porta cabins and threw open the same door as before. The office was as I remembered, but inside sitting at a shabby desk was a portly Asian male in his fifties, wearing a HiViz jacket.

"Can I help you?" he enquired. I ignored him totally, and marched past towards the further door, with Melisa in tow, apologising meekly for the intrusion. I pulled on the further door handle but it would not open.

"Excuse me, this is a private office. What do you want?"

"I want to go in there! I want to see that bloody Doctor!"

"There is no Doctor in there madam."

"Can you open the door please?"

"But there are no Doctors here. I can assure you. The Doctors are over in the hospital"

It was too much. I suddenly screamed at the man insanely, "Open the fucking door! I have been fucking drugged and raped in there! Open it .. NOW!"

The man jumped up in a panic. He hurriedly fumbled about in the desk draw then produced a bunch of keys. He warily strode past the two seemingly insane women in his office, then shaking through the bunch he selected the correct key and unlocked the door. I did not wait for him to open it, and barged past throwing open the door, which to my horror lead directly into a muddy builder's site. Gone was the ornate garden, the water features, the furniture, and the handsome Doctor Sahasrabudhhe. I stood, mouth gaping, staring across the building site.

"It's impossible" I muttered.

"Have you finished here?" said the man nervously. Melisa looked at him, then at me as I stood still, staring into the yard mouth open, eyes wide with confusion. She took control, and quietly ushered me back inside and from the cabin back to the car.

Back inside the safety of the Figaro, Melisa tried to make sense of what had happened. I was dumb struck, but begun to return to reality, although I was still in a high state of confusion.

"What the fuck is going on?"

"You must have been dreaming Eve… and flicking your bean!" Mel giggled.

"Stop it, Mel. It's not funny"

"You must admit, it's actually fucking hilarious. You talk about

Adam wanking in bed, and you're fucking flicking your bean in a car park!"

"Shut up, it's so embarrassing" I began to laugh and relax, believing that somehow I had an intense dream. *'But it was SO real!'*

"Shall we try and find this Doctor then?"

"No, just take me home Mel, I need wine."

"Right, we don't need this then" said Melisa and grabbing the card she ripped it into pieces and tossed it out of the window.

"Don't throw it out on the floor! litter lout!"

"Get you, car park bean flicker and dogger! You can't talk! Let's fuck off, we need a drink. You can tell me all about your sexy dream"

We drove away, with Melisa giggling and chatting about catching me in such a fashion, finding the whole scenarios hilarious. I though sat quietly, my mind in total confusion. If it had indeed been a dream, it was the most intensive one of my life.

But that was all it could have been….

Couldn't it?

6

THE EVIL COCK MONSTER

That night Adam arrived home late. Since the argument he had felt the need to stay away as much as possible to avoid Evette, and a further confrontation.

As he drove up, he saw Melisa's Figaro parked on the drive. Adam liked Melisa but knew if she was still at his house most likely there was some sort of drama, or she would be lying down pissed on his sofa.

On opening the door, he expected Evette to be waiting angrily, demanding why he was late and where he had been, but this occasion she was just sitting alone in the dark of the lounge. The room smelt heavily of Alcohol.

"Hi Eve, are you okay?" he said.

#

I stood slowly, without saying anything. I walked lazily up to Adam, and slumped my head into his chest.

"No, I've had a terrible nasty nasty day."

"Where's Mel?"

"She was pissed so she got an Uber home."

"I think you may be a little worse for wear yourself."

"I am, and … I have been a bitch, haven't I?"

Adam shook his head.

"No, you're just tired. Come on, let me take you to bed."

Adam lifted me, and carried me up the stairs to the bedroom. He laid me softly onto the bed. I was already dressed in a onesie, which often occurred when Mel stayed over too long. Kissing me gently on the forehead, he tucked me in. I turned onto my side, cuddling into my feather pillow and closed my eyes.

"I love you Adam, I promise that I will change."

Adam chuckled gently, "You're fine. See you in the morning."

#

I woke in the early hours of the morning. It was still dark, and I fumbled around looking for the clock. When I could not find it, I realised that I was sleeping on the wrong side of the bed. *Strange.*

I had an urgent need for a pee, so I sat up, and in half sleep, slouched across to the ensuite bathroom. I left the light off as usual so not to wake Adam and pushed the soft touch toilet seat gently down. Turning to sit, I realised that I was not wearing my onesie nor any underwear,.

Slightly puzzled though I was, it was too late in the night to wonder about such things, so I slowly relaxed in order to relieve my bladder. As I did so, instead of the usual trickling of wee in the bottom of the toilet, I was disturbed by a much louder and harsher sound, similar to a water jet. Worse still, I realised that I was actually pissing over the top of the toilet seat onto my lap and the floor. I instinctively pushed my hand into the fountain which was emerging from beneath me, trying to block its path to the tiled floor.

In a panic, I felt down to my crutch, but to my sheer horror, my hand suddenly felt the top of some sort of a creature which was spitting the liquid out. I screamed and looked between my legs, and saw that the wee was not coming from me, but from a huge, deformed, snake like monster in my toilet!

I screamed again, and stood upright, but the monster had attached itself to me, and continued to spray the foul liquid all over the bathroom. I screamed louder, but my voice felt harsh, and strange. I could hear Adam screaming too!

"FUCK! FUCK! HELP HELP! ADAM FUCKING HELP!"

The door to the ensuite flew open and the light suddenly lit the room. "What the fuck are you doing Adam? You're pissing all over the floor!" someone else screamed. I looked up but my sight was distorted by the sudden bright light, but as my eyes cleared I saw a woman standing at the doorway. She looked familiar.. ?

What? wait no... what? Thats ME !!

My mind was now racing in a confused irrational warped state. I was standing in my own bathroom, screaming like a deranged terrified child undergoing a horrific dream, while being scolded by another version of myself, and all my other self could do is complain about the piss on the floor.

"Adam! Adam!" she yelled, "For fuck's sake you're pissing over the fucking floor! Stop!"

Get a grip Evette, you're having a dream, a nightmare. You will wake up... just be...

I was suddenly pushed by this other self and was spun around to face the toilet. The foul liquid from the monster was now bouncing off the inside seat cover back at me. Reaching down I took control of the pissing snake that had attached itself to my crutch, and grabbing its ugly bulbous head I pointed it down towards the toilet bowl. The stiff creature tried to resist, and pushed back but I forced its head down, pointing the stream into the toilet water below. The noise of the liquid hitting the water seemed familiar in a strange sort of way which did not help my confusion. But the more I looked, the more the realisation dawned on me..

It's a cock! I've grown a cock! OH my God! Okay... be calm... you're dreaming, you'll wake up in a minute.

The other Evette continued to fuss around in the ensuite, squirting bleach around the room as she mopped up the wee from the floor.

I lent into the wall above the toilet, head hung low as the evil cock monster finished its endless pissing. I then looked to my left into the mirror but my hair had partially fallen over my eyes. I brushed it back and looked into the eyes of … Adam… standing there.. staring back at me, leaning on one arm over the toilet, just like me…

The dice slowly began to roll, and tumbled into place….

Adam ... I'm Adam ...

"You're sleeping on your own tonight" barked the other Evette before storming off to the guest bedroom.

I turned and stared into the mirror at Adams reflection. It was strange beyond comprehension. I moved my hands like a child trying to out-manoeuvre him, thinking that it might be some clever illusion, but to no avail. I had watched films on the mythical body swap theory, but usually both partners swap bodies, so Adam in theory should be in my body, but evidently he was not.

This is crazy... it can't be real.

As it sunk in, I began to feel faint. Breathing rapidly I sought the stability of the toilet seat, and sat back down. I was desperately trying to calm my heartbeat, well, Adam's heartbeat to be precise! I breathed deeply closing Adam's eyes.

Come on, get a grip Evette, there must be some reasonable explanation.

Then the image and voice of Doctor Sahasrabudhhe drifted into my mind.

"...Would it help if you could. If you were able to see things from his own eyes for instance?"

The fucking bastard! He did this!

I opened Adam's eyes, well now they were my eyes, and I stared down at my new body. I ran my hands over my chest. Gone were the cumbersome boobs, replaced by a tight set of pectoral muscles. I ran my hands over the compact flesh, needing the small, neat nipples with my fingertips, feeling them harden slightly. For a moment, I found myself enjoying the sensation much the same as when I played with my own breasts. When I had breasts that is!

This is so bizarre!

Breathing slower now, I looked down at my now flat and slightly hairy stomach, and further down to… it.

Oh my God ... it's fucking alive..

My new cock has a mind of its own and slowly, it was becoming erect. It looked me directly in the eye and twitched as if to egg me on to play with it.

"God no, fuck that!" I cried standing up in a panic. I grabbed my own dressing gown from the hanger and threw it around Adam's body, but it barely fitted, and my new cock poked its ugly head through the front of the garment.

"Jesus! Has this thing got a mind of its own?"

I threw off my.. well Evette's own gown and hurriedly tried to hang it but I dropped it on the floor in my haste. Bending down to retrieve it, I felt a stiff prod in my stomach. Looking down there was the cock monster staring back at me. Almost winking!

What does it want for Christ's sake? A waggle?

"Oh, fuck off please!" I whined.

Grabbing Adam's dressing gown, I threw it roughly around my shoulders, and marched out of the bathroom leaving Evette's own dressing gown on the floor. I needed to talk to my other self to see if Adam was in there. I stood at the guest room door and knocked gently.

"Adam, are you awake?"

Hang on... I'm Adam!

"Evette are you awake?" I whispered, correcting myself.

"Go away Adam" came the reply from therein.

"I need to talk."

I heard the rustling of bedding followed by disgruntled mumblings. The voice from the bedroom sounded different than my own and was very grumpy. The door opened partially, and I found herself face to face with … myself.

God this is so strange...

I stared at the puckered angry face scowling through the gap in the doorway. It was surreal, unbelievable in every way. Familiar yet different, the voice, the face reversed, hair on the wrong side.

"What? What Adam?"

"Can I come in please Evette? I need to tell you something."

The other Evette turned abruptly and marched back to the bed, jumping in and dragging the bedding high over her chest. She sat there; legs hugged to her chest glaring angrily at Adam… at me.

"Well? What?"

Oh my God I am such a stroppy bitch!

"Something has happened."

"Yes, you pissed all over my floor at three o'clock in the morning. I know, I just cleared it up," she barked.

"No, wait please listen. I don't know how to say this. But are you feeling yourself?"

"No Adam, I'm not. I am stressed beyond belief, I am worried about you, I have had a completely weird day, I think I am having a breakdown mentally and to be honest, it's all your fault."

"What? How?"

"What with your waggling, your constant wanting sex, your refusal to see anyone."

"Yes, yes, I know, but I want to talk about when I, … I mean you, went to see that Doctor yesterday."

The other Evette's eyes shot open wide, her lips drew thin, and she looked at me hard.

"You've been talking to Mel, haven't you? That fucking bitch! I suppose you've both had a great laugh at my expense."

"No, No, I haven't. Look I know it sounds strange but remember when the Doctor..."

"Get out Adam, just get out."

"But he said I... well, you, would understand, that you would understand … Adam."

"I'm not talking about this. Get out! Get out!"

"He changed me into Adam, I am Adam, well, you are Adam inside me!"

The other Evette's screams drowned out my words, there was no getting through. The stress was enormous, and escape was the only answer.

Back in the bedroom, I pondered the unreal situation. I was now Adam, not Evette. Not only did I need to understand Adam, but I also needed to learn to live with her own self.

And that woman, is a complete bitch!

7

ADAM… YOU ARE NOT EVETTE!

The following morning, now in the body of Adam, I was laying in my bed. I could not get up and face the other Evette or the world, as a man. There was too much to learn, too much to try and understand. Living as Adam after years of being Evette just did not comprehend.

How do I shower? How do I go to the toilet? How can I work? I don't know anything about Adam's job.

The bedroom door opened, and the other Evette stormed inside.

"Are you getting up Adam or are you staying here all day stinking the room out?"

I simply rolled into the pillow avoiding the confrontation.

"I'm staying here, I'm ill"

"You're not, there's nothing wrong with you"

If only you knew...

"Well? Are you getting up or not? I've got to get on Adam. Some of us have things to do."

Evette pulled the quilt back fully, exposing my new naked body.

"Yuk!" she exclaimed, "you can cover that up."

I weakly pulled the quilt up, as I pretty much knew what would now happen, and it did. My other self just doggedly dragged the quilt from the bed, followed by the pillows stating that she needed to wash the bedding as my piss ridden body had soiled it the previous night. It was as expected, it was what I myself would do if I were not Adam now. I knew everything about Evette as I was once her, so nothing was a surprise.

I am such a cow ...

I laid there briefly, face and body flat against the bed trying to grab a couple of seconds to regain control, but Evette dragged the sheet from underneath me forcing me to move onto the bare mattress.

"Get in the shower please. Now!" were Evette's parting unsympathetic words.

Like a scolded pup, I slumped into the ensuite bathroom and stared down at my cock which was rising to greet me.

"Oh... you're awake I see. Disgusting thing!"

I slapped the beast hard.

"Ow! Fuck!" I yelled in pain. Surprised at just how sensitive a penis is, I held it briefly for comfort, then the natural disgust of my own side of being Adam took control and I quickly withdrew my hand.

"God I hate you! Filthy snake!"

I looked into the mirror, and spoke to Adam's reflection to gain some composure at the unreal situation.

"Adam.. where are you? Why am I in your body? Speak to me…please!"

I stared into Adam's eyes, trying to see any sort of sign he was in there. *Maybe if I look close enough, a tiny version of him, tapping on the insides of his retinas would appear.*

I listened also for his voice somewhere in my head.. but nothing.. I was alone, and he was lost. I had to get a grip.

"Okay now Evette, pull yourself together. You can do this. Just shower, and then we can go and find that fucking Doctor and sort this all out."

I got into the shower and began to wash my hair, well Adam's hair that is. Firstly, I was surprised to find that I used far too much shampoo, and the bubbles around my head were immense. After rinsing, and conditioning at a more sensible amount, I progressed to washing, and exploring Adams body.

Scrubbing his face, I noticed the roughness of his whiskers in contrast to the softness of his skin. I stroked his cheeks, and then his neck, shoulders, and chest. The hot water splashing over his body made me relax and tingle. It was strange in so many ways. As Evette, I would spend ages on my hair. As Adam I only took a few minutes, and it was done. When it came to washing it was also easy. Instead of having to arduously lift each of my breasts and scrub underneath, I merely ran the soap filled buff puff over his muscular body. I scrubbed around his chest, abdomen, then further downwards from his stomach, then my hand hit something hard.

My God! Does this thing ever rest?

Standing proudly in the air was Adam's cock. Shining brightly in the water, large, swollen, stiff. I grimaced, and roughly poked at the head with the buff puff to clean the filthy thing.

"Ow! Jesus! It's bloody sensitive!"

Dropping the buff puff to the floor of the shower, I took the bar of soap and made a thick lather in my hands. I drew a deep breath, and slowly reached down, grabbing the cock around the neck with a finger and thumb, rubbing soap over the head. The sensation now was at complete opposite to the buff puff's roughness. Immediately I was treated to a deep pleasurable feeling which was strong and gratifying. I carried on tentatively at first, using just my fingertips over the swollen head of the penis. Then I wrapped all my fingers around it and began to rub gently up and down the shaft, then back up to circle the head with my palm and fingers. Every movement sent a wonderful sensation through the tip of my new penis straight to my brain.

This is wonderful...

Instinctively, I began to quicken the pace, my hand now racing up and down the cock. I threw my face into the heat and pulsation of the water, as I waggled furiously, pushing Adam's hips forwards towards the shower wall, back arched, body alive and tense, my head filled with nothing but a driving instinct to keep going no matter what.

"Filthy Dirty Bastard!" Evette's scream brought a sudden end to the pleasure.

"I wasn't doing anything!" I said, turning my back to her to hide the erection.

"Get out Adam! I knew I couldn't trust you" she bellowed, and promptly turned on the hot tap in the sink to full, causing the shower to lose the hot water pressure and showering Adam's naked body in icy cold spray.

"Fuck Evette that's freezing!" I yelled.

"I'm going to Mothers; you can stay here on your own"

My other self slammed the door, leaving me alone and stranded in Adams now cold body, staring down at the now drooping cock.

I began to cry, sobbing uncontrollably, desperate for answers. Desperate for help, but who could I turn to? Who would believe me?

I remained inside the en suite for the next few minutes, sat on the toilet wrapped in a towel staring at Adam's reflection in the mirror. He looked weak, dishevelled, pitiful. Not the man I knew and loved.

What have I done?

Evette's angry unforgiving voice from outside the door broke my silent contemplation.

"I'm going now Adam, are you staying here or what?"

"I'm going in later; I need to rest a bit"

There was no reply other than a series of mutters and grunts from the other Evette, as she quickly exited the bedroom in a huff.

The sound of her car leaving noisily outside prompted me into reluctant action. I stood in front of the mirror once more and pulled Adams body upright.

"We can do this. We just now have to work out how. We need to get you dressed Adam."

I had shaved before, but never my face. I hated the seeing stubble on Adam, and I would tell him that he looked like a tramp whenever he forgot to shave, or couldn't be bothered to do so. Thankfully he used an electric razor, so it shouldn't be too hard. I grabbed his razor, and buzzed it around Adam's face for what seemed like an eternity. No Matter how many times I ran the razor over certain areas, there remained tiny black whiskers that seemed to just laugh at my attempts at man stuff.

Finally satisfied that I had done enough, I put the razor back on the charger and tackled the hair. My own hair would take ages to dry and ages to comb and style, but not Adam's.

Men have it so easy I thought as I quickly blew the hairdryer over Adams short thick hair. I rubbed a small amount of hair putty into my palms as I had seen Adam do so often, and roughly styled his hair to how I liked it. I admired his face in the reflection. He was a very handsome man indeed.

I got dressed in Adam's clothes, picking out my favourite casual outfit from his wardrobe. I admired his good looks from within and staring into the mirror I took out his after shave from his drawer. I poured an amount of *Bleu* by Chanel into the palm of my hand and splashed it over Adam's face.

"Oh Fuck! That stings! Fuck fuck fuck!" I cried, fanning my face frantically. The stinging quickly faded luckily, so I then could enjoy the smell. I had to admit, I quite enjoyed dressing Adam. I felt like a child dressing up, playing Mummies and Daddies, only this time I was the Daddy.

As the hours went by, I began to feel almost at home in my new body. I felt like I had just dressed Adam but did so to my style and satisfaction. I then began thinking that maybe the Doctors intention was not for me to be Adam and understand him, but that he has given me the opportunity to *change* him into my perfect man for when I did turn back to my own body.

"I could do this. I can make you perfect Adam!" I said.

The ringing of the doorbell interrupted my admiration and thoughts. I ran down to the front door and opened it to see Melisa standing there, looking rough and dishevelled.

"Mel! Oh my God, thank God you're here!"

"Err, yes, okay Adam... if you say so. Is Evette here?" said Melisa, slightly confused by my enthusiastic welcome.

"Evette? oh right. You had better come in; I've got something to tell you."

Melisa followed to what she thought was a slightly flapping Adam into the lounge.

"Do you want a drink, Mel? Wine?"

"Oh God no, not this early. Besides, I had a skin full last night with your Mrs. hence my car blocking your drive. Sorry about that Adam"

"No, no don't worry. Look, I don't know how to tell you this but, you remember yesterday?"

Melisa laughed.

"Er yes! It was only yesterday, although the evening got a bit blurred"

"Oh my God, I don't know how to tell you this" I said. I was now beginning to panic, and I could feel myself becoming emotional, and tears were beginning to form in my eyes.

Melisa knew Adam well, but to her he was behaving very oddly, and the absence of Evette, as Melisa knew her, was beginning to sound an alarm.

"What's happened Adam? Is it Evette? Is she okay?"

"No no sorry Mel, she is fine. It's not that exactly"

"Has she left you? Have you fallen out? I know you are having problems but ..."

"No, well yes sort of, but there is more."

My emotions began to overcome me, and I began to cry. Melisa though could only see Adam, a man she had known for years and secretly fancied, crying and behaving totally uncharacteristically.

"Oh My God Adam, come here!"

She stood and embraced Adam's shaking emotional body and sat me on the sofa next to her. She hugged me tightly, kissing his head and pulling him into her bosom. I felt the comfort of the embrace and snuggled into Melisa willingly.

"What is it, Adam? You can tell me."

"I'm not sure how Mel…It's all so weird," I wept.

"Shhh shh Adam. I know... it's okay."

Melisa stroked Adam's hair and brow as I cried softly. She had held a long-standing crush on him and had often fantasised about this moment. Body to body, him vulnerable and available. Hers to explore, abuse, dominate… and if things went according to her fantasy, to fuck. She hugged Adam into her breast, kissing his head several times, and I noticed her breathing intensify as her arousal began to take over.

I suddenly became aware of a difference in Melisa's demeanour. Being her closest friend, I had often exchanged such moments of comfort when had a problem. Hugging was the de-rigour for their relationship, but kissing of heads? I sat bolt upright.

"What are you doing Mel?"

Melisa was taken aback; she could tell that she had overstepped the mark. Perhaps she had miss read the situation.

"Nothing, er sorry Adam, I was just…"

"Sorry nothing Mel! I know what you're doing! You're trying to fuck Adam!"

"Hang on Adam."

"No Melisa! You're out of order, you saw Adam was upset, and you thought you'd try for a sympathy fuck!"

"What? No! Fuck off! Never!"

"Don't lie! I know you fancy him, you said as much before. You said you'd totally fuck him if I remember rightly."

I raised two fingers on both hands, motioning the Speech Mark sign to emphasise my statement.

"I'm going!"

Mel grabbed her bag and stood abruptly. I then panicked.

"What? No no... please! I'm sorry, I'm so fucked up. Please Mel, I need your help. You're the only one I can trust."

Melisa stared at me and Adams face. To her he looked completely lost and in a panic. She was also worried about the absence of Evette and curious about what was going on. She relented and sat back down.

"I'm sorry Mel, I just thought for a minute you wanted to fuck Adam. I just misread the situation."

"Okay... but why are you talking like a professional boxer? In third person? You're not promoting anything here Adam. You're being a bit weird"

"You don't know how weird this is Mel. Promise me. Let me get a drink."

I went into the kitchen and I quickly filled two large crystal goblets with wine, and hurried back to the lounge before Melisa had a chance to run out.

"Ewe, no thanks Adam. It's way too early"

"Trust me, you'll need it in a minute." I assured her.

I placed the drink on the coffee table in front of Mel, and then sat opposite her. I motioned a brief 'cheers', then quickly drank the glass to half empty. I could feel Adam's heart was beating fast, so I breathed deeply in and out to try and slow it down.

"Mel, I want you to just listen, and clear your mind. This is unbelievable what has happened, but you must believe me. Okay? Promise me you'll believe me"

"I don't know what you're going to say Adam! How can I promise to believe you?"

I drew a further long deep breath to calm myself.

Easy Evette, take your time, don't fuck this up.

"Yesterday, Mel, we, well no I mean you and Evette went to see a doctor."

"Yes… why? What's happened?"

"Well, I think Evette did see that Doctor."

"Sorry Adam, you're not making sense."

"What I'm trying to say is… somehow, Evette did see the Doctor."

"Well, since you mention it, and Evette has obviously told you I'm guessing. We went to see him, but no one had heard of him. So we came away basically. Why are you mentioning this?"

"You're not going to believe this Mel"

I began to panic, as Adam's pulse began to race even harder, and his breath quickened. I frantically gulped down the glass of wine.

"Jeez Adam, you're starting to freak me out now." said Mel.

"Look, there is no easy way to tell you this, but I … am Evette."

I paused, expecting some sort of astonishing reaction from Mel, but instead she simply rolled her eyes to one side, and hung her mouth open as if she was straining to think of a sensible reply.

"Adam... you are not Evette." she said eventually.

"I am... Inside! That Doctor yesterday, he was real. He has changed me into Adam!"

Mel stared at me, mouth open, eyes wide trying to contemplate that her best friend's husband has gone completely mental.

"It's me Mel! I'm Eve! I'm trapped in Adam's body! That fucking Doctor has somehow changed me!" I yelled.

"Oh, fuck off Adam!"

"I'm not fucking Adam! I'm me! I'm Evette!"

Melisa grabbed her bag and stood abruptly,

"I'm leaving, this is too fucking weird Adam. You've seriously got issues"

She began to walk out, but I stood infant of her and grabbed her by both arms.

"No, please Mel wait. I know this is strange, I can't fucking believe it myself. Please listen, hear me out, I'm going out of my fucking mind here. Please!"

Mel tried to free herself, but Adam's grasp was too firm.

"Fucking let me go Adam. Now!"

She struggled abruptly pulling and twisting her arms to get free. I saw the fear growing in my friend's face, so I released my grip slowly, not realising the strength of Adam's hands. Melisa pulled away and stared at Adam's face, which was drawn of colour, torn, sad, and broken. Not the man she knew at all. She turned and walked towards the door, but Adam's final plea stopped her.

"Please Mel... I need help. You're all I have, don't go…. Please."

Mel had never seen him like this. Despite Evette's absence she could not desert him now. She turned and faced him.

"Okay Adam, you talk, and I'll listen, but you touch me again…"

"I won't. Just hear me out please." I begged.

She returned to the sofa and sat while I went through the whole story, including every detail of Dr Sahasrabudhhe, his consultation, his love making and my waking to find myself alone masturbating in the Figaro. Melisa sat eyes wide, intently listening to every word. And also secretly feeling slightly aroused at Adam's detailed description of Evette's seduction by the Doctor.

When I told her about waking in the night and going to the toilet as Adam, Mel actually burst into giggles, causing a similar reaction in me. Whatever she thought Adam was on, was very entertaining for Mel, if weird.

"We need more wine," I said, pausing for refreshment. To her surprise Mel had unwittingly drunk the entire contents of her glass too. I quickly topped up both glasses to the brim, and then took a large drink. Melisa, probably due to the bizarre circumstances, did the same.

"Oh my God, where was I?"

"In the shower, with a hard on." giggled Mel.

"Oh... yes, well let's skip that bit. But what I am trying to tell you Mel, is that somehow overnight. that fucking Doctor has changed me into Adam. And.." seriously.. I don't know what to do. Help me.. please."

Mel just sat quietly. She didn't know what to say. My story had ended, but the conclusion was still unbelievable, and probably impossible for Mel to comprehend.

Why the fuck is he saying this? What is his game? She thought.

"Look Adam..."

"Mel! Have you not heard me? I am Eve! You know! Evette! Your best friend! Your confidant! I am trapped in Adam's body!"

"Look, I get what you're saying Adam..."

That was it, she wasn't getting me so I shouted loudly "EVETTE! MY FUCKING NAME IS EVETTE!"

"Okay okay! ... Christ! This is pretty fucking weird"

"You're telling me? I know how fucking weird this is Mel!"

"Okay, look. I have listened to you now can I just say something without you shouting Ad'... sorry. Eve?"

I nodded, keeping Adam's mouth tightly shut to try not to scream at my friend.

"As much as you tell me, and quite honestly you have described every detail of yesterday quite accurately, you could have gotten all this from Evette this morning, and for some reason, I don't know why exactly, you are telling me all this"

"Why Mel? Why would I make this all up?"

"I don't know, maybe you're ill, or you've banged your head, or had a brain fuck or something."

"No, how would I know about me masturbating in the Figaro? You know that I would never admit to that. Especially to Adam!"

She had a point thought Melisa, *hang on ... he had a point!* It began to dawn on Melisa that Adams mannerisms, speech rhythm and demeanour was uncannily like that of Evette.

Can this be real?

"Okay, answer this, what is my pet hate?" she said.

"That's easy, burping. Adam probably knows that Mel. Ask me another, something only you and me would know"

"Okay, who was the teacher we both fancied in the 4th year?"

"Mr Cole, we both loved his long blonde hair and blue eyes. Ask me another."

"Er … who wanked off David Archer in the girl's toilets?"

"You did, you dirty bitch. Adam would know that too Mel, he went to our school. What about me and you. Something only we would know?"

Melisa stared; her eyes began to widen.

"Okay, what is the worst thing you and I have ever done? Or if you like you in particular have done?"

I felt decidedly uncomfortable at Mel's question and lowered my gaze from Melisa's probing eyes.

"I licked your Virginia when you were sleeping!" I said quietly.

There followed several seconds silence as Mel took the sentence in. She suddenly recalled a sleepover at Evette's where they shared the same bed, and she woke in a half dream about her and Evette having oral sex. She remembered accusing Evette of it on that night believing that she had woken during the act, but she was eventually convinced the whole thing was a dream by Evette's denials at the time. It was the first time Evette had admitted what Mel had always suspected.

It can't be.. but only Evette would know that.. but it can't be.. can it?

Mel stared at me, for what seemed ages. She seemed to be going over the absurd scenario again and again. Looking at me. Looking at my hands, how I held my glass, how I sat, how I spoke. My expressions, diction, mannerisms all screamed Evette yet my body was obviously that of Adam. I could see her face change as she slowley began to believe me.

"Oh my God… Evette! It is you! You're really... Jesus Christ! I can't take this in. It's really you"

I nodded; tears started flowing from my eyes. I began sobbing with relief as Melisa stood and embraced Adam's body.

"I believe you Eve, I believe you. I'm sorry"

She hugged Adam's body, but she now could see into the eyes of Evette.

"Now we have to work out what to do" she said.

Melisa's phone rang, she glanced across to see it was Evette calling. As strange as this whole situation was, she ignored her best friend on the phone to concentrate on her other friend, trapped in the body of her husband.

"That's you calling Evette, well you as in the other you"

"Ignore her, she's just being a bitch, just hug me, I need it" I said.

We remained in the embrace, both enjoying the closeness and security that only a hug can provide. That is until I felt pressure in an unfamiliar area of my body, as Melisa's embrace began to turn into a grinding session.

I pulled away sharply from Melisa, "What the fuck Mel? You're rubbing your crutch against me!"

Melisa scowled "Hang on Adam, you're the one with the fucking hard on!"

I looked down at Adam's crutch, sure enough I could see the outline of his erection fully from under his jeans. Briefly lost for words, I turned away from Mel, "This fucking thing! It has a mind of its own."

Looking back at Melisa, I also noticed Adam's gaze also had a mind of its own, as I found myself staring at Melisa's breasts. Quickly lifting my eyes, I looked directly into the eyes of Mel, but could feel Adam's face reddening slightly. I also noticed a mischievous look in Melisa's face.

"What Mel?"

"Have you tried it?"

"What? Tried what?"

"You know, your new cock?"

"What? NO fuck off!"

"You're joking! If I had a cock suddenly, I'd wank the fuck out of it!"

"Mel!" I exclaimed, shocked and slightly disgusted at the

suggestion, "That's disgusting!"

"Oh, come on! Surely you must have wondered what it must feel like. I have."

"Never!" I snapped haughtily, "and besides, it's none of your business."

"Come on Eve, look at it. It's almost bursting through your jeans."

I glanced down at Adams crutch. The bulge was there for all to see. I was embarrassed but I also felt incredibly aroused by the whole situation.

"It just needs a wee." I said and hurried off to the toilet leaving Melisa alone.

"Have a wank!" cried Melisa as I departed the room.

#

Once she heard his footsteps run upstairs Melisa sat back on the sofa and pushing her hand down into the front of her jeans, she laid back, closed her eyes, and began gently stroking herself under her panties.

I'm going to...

8

THE OTHER EVETTE

Evette sat in her car outside her mother's house, staring at her iPhone after another attempted call to Melisa was apparently being ignored.

She is probably still sleeping, lazy cow she thought, presuming her to be out of reach due to her intoxicated state last night.

Melisa's answerphone announced her as unable to reach the phone, causing Evette to abruptly hang up. She stared at the front door of the large, impressive house that used to be her happy family home for many years. Although she was close to her mother in many ways, she preferred to keep a distance where issues of her and Adam's relationship were concerned. Still, she had to start somewhere, and her mother would have to do for now.

Leaving the car, she took a deep breath, and strode up the gravelled driveway to the grand double fronted entrance door. Glancing up at the CCTV cameras as she approached, she could not help feeling annoyed by her mother not being there standing at the open door to welcome her in. She had already been granted entrance through the gated driveway, by a rude and unfriendly buzz rather than any verbal welcome from the occupant who would clearly know the identity of the visitor.

Nevertheless, it was time to get into character. If Evette expected any amount of sympathy from her mother that is. She thought hard about the prospect of her, and Adam's marriage ending and willed a tear to appear in her eye. Feeling suitably upset, she pressed the button on the RING security front doorbell and stood staring at the Fisheye camera lens waiting for the door to be opened. A familiar voice crackled over the speaker.

"Can I help you?"

Evette drew a sharp breath, annoyed at her mother's game.

"It's me Mother! Open the door please"

A buzzing rang out, and a loud click as the electric door lock was released from within. Evette pushed on the heavy door and stepped into the large hallway. Of course, there was no one to greet her. Her mother was elsewhere in her palace, probably still in bed.

"Mother!" she called.

There was no reply, Evette removed her shoes, and deposited her bag on the Chaise Longue. Checking her reflection in the mirror, she saw that she had an air of dishevelled distressed daughter in her persona, but the effects of her self-induced tear jerking were wearing thin.

"Mother! Where are you?"

Her mother's voice replied from the back of the house.

"I'm in the garden room"

Evette walked briskly through the grand hallway, through the Victorian Flair designer lounge to the garden room. There, amongst the luxury orangery furniture, flowing grape vines hanging from the ceiling rafters, and huge Mandevilla, Bougainvillea, and Hoya shrubs growing from matching planters sat her mother.

Seated on a yoga mat in the dead centre of the room, eyes closed, mind focused, she paid no heed to her daughter's entrance. The sound of mindfulness Hindu spiritual music played from a smart speaker on the side table, as she breathed deeply in meditation.

"Mother!"

Her mother raised a hand abruptly indicating that it was not the time for any disturbance.

"Mother! Please!" retorted Evette, "I need to talk to you. Now!"

Evette's mother looked slowly over her shoulder at her daughter, her face displaying impatience at the intrusion. But on seeing Evette's tearful eyes, reddened cheeks and slightly dishevelled hair resulted in the desired reaction.

"Oh sweety, you're upset!"

Taking her cue, Evette dropped her shoulders, pushed out her bottom lip, then using her inner child she staggered over to her mother, arms outstretched sobbing.

Uncomfortable with emotions, her mother stayed seated in "Lotus Pose" while Evette stooped low giving her mother an ill received awkward hug.

"There there..." she said, patting Evette's back firmly before standing abruptly to avoid the embrace as much as possible. "Now stop all that nonsense and tell me what's wrong"

"it's Adam, I think we've broken up"

"Huh, I can't say that I am surprised"

"What? Why?"

"I never thought he'd stay; he has a wandering eye that one"

"Mother! He'd never be unfaithful!" said Evette "Why would you think that?"

"Men are all the same, they can't get enough sex, so they look elsewhere"

Evette was slightly shocked at her mother's opinion of Adam. *Surely, he wouldn't*

"He's not like that, it's different. It's something he did"

"Then tell me"

It dawned on Evette suddenly, that perhaps her mother wasn't the right person to have this discussion with. After all, she was never one for compassion, and criticism was her usual input whenever Evette went to her with a problem.

"I can't, it's too embarrassing"

"If he's not being unfaithful then, is it money?"

"No, we have plenty of money"

"Then it's sex then, it's either one or the other" said her mother impatiently. "It's all your father and I ever argued about, though mostly about sex"

"Mum! Please don't talk about dad's and yours sex life!"

Her mother laughed, "We did have sex Evette! How do you think we had you?"

"It's not sex, we have sex. But I think…" she paused in her own thoughts briefly, "he doesn't want a baby"

Evette's own words were unexpected, and up until that point she hadn't thought that the problem with Adam would have anything to do with their decision to have children.

Oh my God! That is why he waggles; he's trying to not get me pregnant!

The thought overwhelmed her and she began to cry again, for real this time. Not just for attention.

That explains everything!

Her mother quickly put an arm around Evette and guided her to the sofa. She knew how important having a child was to her daughter, much more than she herself had ever felt.

"I'm so sorry Evette, I didn't realise. Has he said this to you?"

Evette shook her head.

"So how do you know?"

"I can't say"

"I can't help you Evette if you don't"

Evette looked into her mother's eyes, and for once she could see genuine compassion there. Uninhibited by her usual reluctance to discuss matters of sex with her mother, Evette spoke openly.

"He plays with himself, constantly!"

Her mother felt her face tighten, along with an overwhelming urge to laugh out loud. Holding the urge, she tried to sound sincere and controlled.

"Men do! Well, apparently, they do. It wasn't something your father and I discussed. But men are certainly more needy than women in that respect"

"But not when we are trying to make a baby. He is wasting it deliberately, squirting future generations down the toilet! Our babies!"

It was too much to bear, her mother burst out laughing.

"Mother! It's not funny! Bloody Katrina laughed at me too!"

"You saw Katrina? And you bothered a busy Doctor with that? Really my girl, I thought you were naive, but this is frankly ridiculous"

"Oh my God mother! You really are no help whatsoever!"

Evette rose sharply and marched from the room in a full huff. Grabbing her bag from the chaise longue, she departed, slamming the heavy door behind her.

"Cold hearted cow!"

Returning to her car, Evette rang Melisa's phone again, but no reply. After a couple of attempts she gave up.

She had no choice now; she would have to go home and face Adam.

9

OH MY GOD! OH MY GOD!

I sat in the toilet staring down at the huge penis jutting from the front of Adam's jeans. I could not understand the shortness of breath I was suffering, the racing of Adam's heartbeat in his chest, the strange urge to do something... odd.

I grabbed the hard penis with my finger and thumb, trying to force it downwards towards the water at the bottom of the toilet.

It must need to pee...

Holding it firmly I tried to force it somehow to go, but it just would not co-operate. However, I also felt an overwhelming urge to pull the foreskin back over the swollen tip, and then forward again. It felt satisfying, sensual.

Maybe it needs a massage to start peeing...

I sat back, losing my grip slightly and the penis shot upright defiantly.

Oh my god, this bloody thing...

Grabbing the cock hard this time, I thought that maybe I was being too gentle.

Okay, so you want it rough, do you?

Gripping it hard in my full palm, I pointed the penis downwards again. The foreskin rolled back over the head, it felt nice, I pushed it forwards… then back... then forward again. I closed my eyes, laid back against the seat cover, ignoring the lack of comfort to Adam's back. I knew what I was now doing, but I didn't care. I rubbed faster, and faster! I could not stop!

"Oh my God" I whispered, "this is so wrong."

I could hear Adam's heart beating now, but the only feeling was a rising pressure in his groin. It was like a beautiful strong tickling sensation initially but grew and grew! Building ever stronger as I rubbed faster and harder along the shaft of Adam's cock!

"Oh my GOD!"

The feeling that Adam's whole lower body was about to burst into an incredibly pleasurable eruption encapsulated me.

"OH MY GOD! OH MY GOD!" I screamed, now in a frenzy of pure hard desire. The intense pressure was now firmly in the head of Adam's penis! It was swollen incredibly, and almost deep purple in colour. I stared at it as I rubbed it furiously, out of control and free of all my past inhibitions of touching it before. The deep overwhelming rush of pleasure was now too much. I screamed loudly, arching my back, pushing my hips forwards as I did.

"OH, MY FUCKING GOD!"

Adam came in floods. I could not stop it; I did not want too. I came up everywhere, over Adam's hand, jeans, the wall! Everywhere!

#

Downstairs Melisa could hear everything, but she did not care, the screams of Evette in Adam's body gave her all the excitement she needed, as she too masturbated furiously in the lounge chair. They came together, but apart. Satisfied Melisa quickly pulled her jeans up. Straightening herself she quickly ran up the stairs.

"Evette! Where are you?"

I sat motionless on the toilet, still breathless from the sensual release on Adam's body.

"I'm in our bathroom Mel."

Melisa ran quickly into the bedroom and opened the en-suite door, to see Adam sat on the toilet, his jeans half pulled to his thighs, his half erect penis laying along his lap, which was wet with cum.

I stared slowly at Melisa, head slightly to one side, looking moderately intoxicated.

"Oh, my fucking God, Mel!"

Melisa stared briefly, unsure of what to say.

"Put your fucking cock away Eve!" she giggled, "I take it you tried it out then"

I stood and quickly dressed Adam, not that I cared that Melisa could see him half naked. I felt euphoric.

"Oh my God Mel, no wonder he likes to do that. It was amazing!"

"What did it feel like?"

"I don't know how to describe it really. It was just so intense, sort of primeval." I said, still trying to catch my breath.

"Is it like normal coming? Like you normally do it?"

"It was at the beginning I think, but then it was so strong, it blew my mind to be honest. I have never had that with anyone, not that strong"

"I have" giggled Mel, "With you just now"

"What?"

"Yeah! Really! When you went upstairs, I was proper horny, and I guessed you might have a wank, so I took advantage and had one myself."

"Mel! You didn't"

"Yeah, I did! And when I heard you coming, I proper came! I don't think I have ever been so turned on during a hand job!"

"Dirty bitch!" I giggled.

I started to regain my composure, and thoughts of Adam's semen splashed around the bathroom, and all over his clothes required some immediate action. I quickly removed Adam's clothing, forgetting entirely that Melisa was standing there enjoying the view. I jumped into the shower, standing back as the water warmed before standing under the firm torrent of hot water. The sensation was pleasurable, and as I washed Adam's hair, my mind drifted back to the masturbation moment on the toilet. The same horny sensation began to float into my mind as before, causing the same bodily reaction. Grabbing the soap, I lathered up Adam's hands well, before beginning to gently wash Adam's cock. It was rock hard again.

"Bloody hell, this thing is insatiable!" I said loudly. I looked to my right to see Mellissa was now perched on the floor next to the bath, only a few inches away from me. Her gaze was directly at Adams hot throbbing cock.

"Can I suck it?" she said with a broad hungry grin.

"No, you fucking can't!"

"Eve, I'm not being funny, you have the opportunity to really learn everything about a man. You need to know what it all feels like. Then if you get back to being you, you can totally have the best fucking sex ever! Adam won't know what's hit him!"

I thought briefly, she does have a point, and I am curious to know how it feels...

"No, it wouldn't be right. You're my best friend"

"And? Who better to do it then?"

"I couldn't do it to Adam"

I could Eve! And totally fuck him... thought Mel.

"I understand if you don't want too Evette, believe me, but this is a one-off chance. You might turn back to yourself tomorrow. It's not like I am doing it for me"

I totally am ...

"Besides, you must be curious, surely?"

I was. I could feel Adam's sexual desire taking over my mind. It was so bizarre, the whole situation. Here I was, trapped in my husband's body, not knowing where he was. I was married to my other self, and now about to have a blow job from my best friend.

What the hell, in for a penny...

"Okay, just for a bit" I said, my voice quivering with anticipation.

Melisa needed no further invitation; she stood and quickly began undressing.

"Mel! What are you doing?"

"I'm getting in the shower with you of course. You're soaking wet, and I'm not getting my clothes soaked by you or being covered in your cum thanks"

In seconds she had removed her clothes except for her bra and panties. I could not take Adam's eyes from Melisa's small yet perfect breasts as she removed her laced bra. Bending down to remove her panties, she stood briefly staring at the body of Adam, standing naked, water running down his muscular body, his large erection standing tall waiting for her. This was a moment to savour.

Melisa stepped into the shower, then pushed herself tightly against Adam's body pinning me completely back against the wall.

I weakly complained, "What are you doing Mel?"

"Shut up Eve" said Melisa, then grabbing his cock hard, she kissed Adam's mouth, then neck, chest and ever downwards towards his loins.

I could not resist, and enjoyed every embrace, every moment, every tingle which was enhanced by the hot waters flowing gently down Adam's back, adding to the sensations of pleasure.

Melisa knelt down before me, one hand slowly running up and down Adam's shaft, while the other ran around his muscular buttocks, and under his balls tickling gently around his perineum area. She began kissing the length of his erection from the base, then took the head in her mouth, sucking hard as she did so, allowing her lips to slide back and forth over the head of his cock.

It was heaven, I felt every sensation of Adam's body. His knees began to weaken, and I reached forward to try and support his muscular frame.

"Turn around Mel, so I can hold onto the wall, my fucking knees are going!"

Grinning Melisa happily obliged, turning with her back against the shower wall she hungrily took Adam's cock in her mouth again, her head bobbing back and forth giving me the upmost pleasure.

Using both hands to prop Adam's body up, I stood braced, tense and in total ecstasy. The sensation from Adam's was like that of when he came, but softer and longer. My mind was awash with desire, as the hot water poured over Adam's head and down his back. The deep tickling effect in his loins began growing rapidly towards the build-up of Adams climax.

"I'm going to cum!" I whispered loudly.

"No, you're fucking not!" said Melisa, then standing she pushed Adam's body back and around, then lifted one leg high wrapping it around Adam's waist.

"What are you doing Mel?" I said weakly.

"You're totally gonna fuck me" she said, grabbing Adams hard cock and pushing it deeply inside her. Clamping her arms around Adam's broad shoulders, she whispered into his ear, "Come on, Fuck me. Fuck me hard!"

Instinctively I began thrusting hard deep into Mel, I could not stop. The thought just did not register, I was trapped in passion. I could hear Adam's voice grunting and half growling with lust. Melisa responded with her own loud moans of pleasure, each growing louder and louder with every hard thrust of Adam's body.

"Ah! Ahhh! You're rubbing my clit! You're rubbing my clit! Yes! Yes! YES!" cried Melisa loudly.

"Ah! Ah Hah! I'm gonna cum! I'm gonna cum!" I cried in unison.

"I'm coming I'm coming!" screamed Melisa.

We came together in a crescendo of loud cries and wails, but a louder, harsher, piercing angry scream overcame ours.

"*AHHHH!* WHAT THE FUCK? MEL! YOU BITCH!"

I opened Adam's eyes and looked in the direction of the shouting, straight into the harsh glaring angry eyes of my other self.

"Adam! I might have fucking known! And with her? Really?" she screamed.

Melisa was already out of the shower, hastily grabbing her clothes as she ran past the angry Evette.

I looked at my other self from the eyes of Adam and I felt his heart breaking. I had fucked up, fucked everything up. Even if I did see Doctor Sahasrabudhhe, and he put me back fully into my own body, surely now I had lost Adam for ever.

"I'm sorry Eve, I don't know what to say" I said.

"Don't say anything Adam, just get out of my house. I can't believe it, but my fucking mother was right."

"Mother? Right about what? What has she been saying?"

"Just get out Adam, Get OUT!" screamed the other Evette hysterically.

I grabbed a towel from the rail, wrapping it around Adam's waist, then hurried into the bedroom to grab some clothes. My other self simply regained her dignity, walked past her husband and left the room.

Sitting on the edge of the bed, I stared into the mirror at Adam's saddened face gazing back at me.

"What are we going to do Adam? ..... And what did my fucking mother say?"

I quickly dressed Adam in fresh clothes and tidied the bathroom, whilst my other self remained downstairs, sobbing loudly. Not knowing exactly what to do, I thought it be better to go out for a while until things calmed down. There wasn't any point in trying to explain what had just happened. However, no matter how I looked at it, it was wrong.

Pausing briefly in the lounge I thought to check that my other self was okay. She sat in the armchair, hugging her knees to her chest, rocking slightly. I walked tentatively towards her, but she refused to look in my direction.

"Are you alright?" I said softly. It was odd, even though I really did not know my own self from another perspective, I instinctively could feel Adam's hurt at seeing his partner in this way.

"Go away Adam, I can't talk to you now"

"Please Evette, let me explain"

"JUST FUCK OFF ADAM! FUCK OFF!" she screamed, "I can't talk to you right now. Just go!"

I knew my own self better than anyone. I knew exactly what she was going to do. In truth she and I had prepared for this day. Mainly due to our awkward sex life, we always half expected him to be unfaithful at some stage. So we previously planned for when he did. My other self would surely contact the family solicitor, then cancel Adam's bank cards, get the family locksmith to change the locks on the house, and start filing for divorce.

The only fly in the ointment is Evette had never prepared for Melisa to be the other woman. Now neither of us had a best friend to lean on.

There was no one to turn to...

Except maybe… my mother.

10

I KNOW WHAT YOU NEED ADAM

Driving to mother's house in Adam's car my mood ran wildly between anger about what she may have said to my other self, and worry about how I would tell my mother what has really happened to me. My anger was not helped by the fact that I can barely drive a manual car, and driving , or attempting to drive Adam's beloved Mini Cooper S was proving to be a bloody nightmare. Crunching through the gears, stalling and Kangeroo-ing aside, I needed to plan my meeting with mother carefully.

How would she react when Adam turns up on her doorstep? Especially as it was obvious that she and my other self had been discussing Adam just prior to her catching me and Mel together. And what if the my other self has already phoned mother about Adam shagging Mel in the shower? What would she say to that? But there was only one way to find out, I had to go and face the music.

If I could learn how to drive this fucking car properly.

#

Pressing on the gate intercom, I soon heard mother's voice crackle over the speaker, "Oh Adam, what can I help you with?"

She sounds guilty... I thought.

"Can we talk mother?"

"I am rather busy... but okay"

The gate slowly opened, and I drove in.

She's definitely guilty! I thought angrily. But I would have to remain calm. To my mother I was Adam, not Evette this time.

My mother and Adam had a frosty relationship at best, so I was not expecting a welcome mat to be thrown out as I arrived. But I needed to find out what mother had said to my other self if I was going to have any chance of saving our marriage.

As I got out of the car mother was already standing at the door. She was almost dressed scantily in tight fitting Daquini yoga pants and vest. She has a youthful yet full figure, and has quite a large bust, which was practically on full display under the bra top. But to me she was dressed quite inappropriately for meeting Adam, so I felt compelled to comment.

"Mother er... you're clearly not ready, would you like to change first?"

"What? Sorry Adam, what do you mean?"

I paused, realising that mother had no idea that she was actually talking to her own daughter in Adam's body. It would not be appropriate for Adam to comment on her mother's attire, no matter how inappropriate that attire was!

"Oh, er nothing mm.." I stuttered. It was also not usual for Adam to address my mother as mother!

"Nothing Pamela" I said.

"To be frank Adam, I half expected you to come here. You know Evette has been here this morning I take it?"

"Yes, and to be honest, I need to know what she has said to you"

"She has said plenty, including the fact that you shagged her best friend in the shower Adam! What the hell are you up too?"

Fuck!

Pamela frowned "But I'm not at liberty to discuss what Evette has said in confidence Adam! Perhaps you should see a solicitor"

"No, no I understand that, but I really need help. I have to talk to someone, please?" I felt a sudden rush of emotion, and tears filled Adam's eyes. Mother stared momently at me, tight mouthed and unwelcoming, but then pulled the door fully open.

"You had better come in Adam"

She led me to the garden room at the rear of the house, and motioned for me to sit on the sofa.

"Would you like a drink Adam?"

I nodded, "Water thanks."

Pamela laughed briefly, "I thought you would have wanted something stronger, under the circumstances."

Stopping at the decanter of Jack Daniels Number seven on the side unit, she selected two crystal tumblers and poured two good measures into each glass.

"Make yourself comfortable, I'll fetch some ice."

Mother glided out of the room, leaving me in a quandary. In an effort to gain comfort, I desperately wanted to tell all to her, but how would she react? The whole situation was so bizarre.

Mother would never believe it.

She returned to the garden room with an ice bucket, and half-filled each glass with ice.

"On the rocks Adam?"

Unsure what Adam would do, I accepted the drink from mother, but held the glass close to Adam's chest.

"Thanks mum."

"Mum?" laughed Pamela "That's a little formal Adam."

"Sorry... Pamela."

"Never mind, now drink up, and tell me what has happened between you two."

As much as I wanted to control myself, I burst into tears. Closing Adam's eyes as I put the glass down and simply sobbed, covering Adam's face to try and hide away from mother's sarcastic judgemental gaze. The next unexpected thing I felt was my mother sitting next to me on the sofa, and placing an arm around Adams shoulders. She pulled me close into her bosom.

"Hey, hey Adam, shh now."

Much to my surprise, she hugged Adam close, rocking him slightly, stroking his hair, and kissed him on the top of his head. It was just what I needed. I felt the release of emotions pour from my soul.

Unable to speak I simply sobbed more for a couple of minutes. Neither of us said anything as mother hugged me close, something she had not done for years. I felt myself calming now, as she gently comforted me. She moved slightly, and guided Adam's head into her lap where I enjoyed her gentle caresses on Adam's hair.

"Now Adam" she said gently, "tell me exactly what has happened."

I thought for a minute. Should I continue as Adam, or try and explain the situation to her? I decided to try and do both perhaps, as I remained in her embrace summoning the courage to speak.

"I don't know where to start, what did Evette tell you?"

"Well, it might be embarrassing for you to talk about that Adam. Are you sure? It is very personal."

I had to know and nodded in mother's lap.

"She said that you and she were having problems, of the intimate kind."

"We are, but she doesn't understand me."

"Women rarely do understand their husbands Adam, and vice versa... She also thinks that you don't want a child, and you are just going along with it to get sex."

I was slightly shocked for some reason, even though Evette's thoughts were truthfully my own, but in Adam's body, they were wrong.

"What? That's nonsense. Why would she say that?" I whined, "We are trying for children at the moment."

"Well." Pamela paused, "I'm not sure you would want me to tell you that."

I tried to sit up, but mother pressed down slightly on Adam's head, and continued stroking his hair.

"Hush Adam, you need to relax."

I snuggled back into mother's lap.

"Evette says that you, well… masturbate constantly Adam, is that true?"

"No, well, not all of the time, but she doesn't understand, it's normal."

Again, after only having only recently discovered the pleasures of male masturbation, I already had a different view now from my other self.

Mother replied, "I know, I know, but Evette doesn't. She is slightly prudish I'm afraid."

"I know that now, but how can I convince her to accept me? She makes me feel so ashamed."

"Don't feel ashamed, it is perfectly normal for a man to do that. You have needs don't you Adam?"

"I do, sometimes it is almost impossible to control."

Mother began stroking Adam's hair and brow again, but her other hand started gently massaging his arm, back and shoulder. I did not notice immediately, as my mind was concentrating on my other self's misinterpretation of trying for a baby.

"How often are you playing with yourself Adam?"

"Not all the time, but when I get in the shower, and wash, it starts, or when I am on the toilet, or like today, when I cuddled Mel.

I really don't know what causes it, but my penis takes over." I said truthfully, still sobbing slightly.

"I understand, I really do. It's not your fault."

She is being really understanding...

"I know now, Adam can't help it. It's not his fault." I whimpered.

"I know dear, I know. I just wish I could help you with it."

"So do I."

Mother continued caressing Adam's head, and upper body, "Does this help Adam?"

I nodded, enjoying the rare display of love from my mother. It was just what I wanted, and I closed Adam's eyes.

Mother gently placed her hand under Adam's cheek, and lifted his head from her lap, I just followed along.

"I know what you need Adam." whispered mother, gently turning Adam's head to face her.

What the FUCK???

I could not believe my eyes! There, less than millimetres from Adam's face were mother's bare breasts. Her yoga bra was pulled high, and both her drooping tits were on full display. She tried to pull Adam's head into her breasts, causing me to recoil sharply and I almost dove away screaming loudly, "MOTHER! HOW COULD YOU?"

Making no attempt to cover up, mother simply scoffed.

"Adam, what do you expect? You are not the only person here with needs. I am a woman too."

"No! You're my fucking mother. Mother!... Mother!!!"

She frowned deeply, and hurriedly pulled the bra top back down.

"No wonder Evette is mixed up. You are obviously gay Adam."

WHAT???

I was shocked, no worse than that. Traumatised! Not only had my own mother tried to cop off with my husband, but now she was accusing him of being gay!

"Gay? Hang on!"

Mother stood sharply and began hurrying for the front door.

"You'd better go Adam. Before I say something that I might regret."

I followed after her, slightly dumfounded for a moment.

"What? How dare you mother!"

She stopped and gave me a smug stare.

"How dare I? How dare you, Adam. You torment my daughter over her wanting a child, and make her miserable, then you come here and try to take advantage of a vulnerable lonely widow."

"Me? Take advantage of You?"

"Yes! You should be ashamed of yourself. You are disgusting!"

I could not believe it. Could this day get any more bizarre? Mother opened the front door wide and stood back glaring at me.

"Now. Get Out! Before I call the police."

"Don't worry, I'm going Mother!" I screamed, and marched out, truly disgusted at her attempt to seduce her son in law, and my husband!

I jumped in the mini, and looked back but mother had already shut the door. Once again, I was lost and alone.

Where would I turn now?

11

IT WASN'T ME

I drove from mother's with my mind in turmoil, as my mood swung erratically between anger and sadness. I found it hard enough to drive Adam's car when I wasn't stressed, but with all this going on I was fearful of crashing unless I calmed Adam's body down.

Pulling over in a lay-by, I stopped to regain my thoughts. *How can I get back to normality now?*

My best friend has done a runner and won't answer her phone, my mother has tried to shag my husband, and God knows what has actually happened to Adam? He must still be in this body with me somehow, as he certainly wasn't in my other self. Emotion again overwhelmed me, and I cried at the thought. I really missed him and longed to talk to him again.

Adam's phone rang interrupting my thoughts. Fumbling in his tight jeans, I clumsily pulled it from the pocket to see a photo of a bearded man and the name 'Rich' filling the screen. It was his close friend Richard from his work. I hesitated, but this was the fifth missed call from him that day. I gathered myself and answered, "Hello?"

"Ad's ? You alright mate? You're supposed to be here helping me on this project presentation. We really need it done today."

"Sorry er.. Richard, but I have gone sick today."

"Sick? What's up? You fucking poof!"

Richard was not the most 'P.C' amongst Adam's friends.

"Oh, nothing serious," I said, unsure exactly why I was speaking to Richard anyway.

"Well, if you're not that ill get in mate, we've got to get this done."

"I can't I'm afraid, it's complicated."

"What are you talking about Adam? How complicated can it be?"

I hesitated. I knew Richard quite well, having met him a few times at Adam's work do's, but not well enough to tell him what really had happened. But also I did not want to get Adam into more trouble. A thought crossed my mind, maybe Richard could help? At least I could get an opinion of someone who knew Adam in a different way. Maybe he would have an idea of how to try and fix this?

"Look, can we meet somewhere Richard?"

"Can't you come in?"

"No, I'm… not myself today."

"Fucking hell, you're not kidding! Look, meet me at Costa's in half an hour."

"Which one?" I asked , as I was unsure of where Adam's workplace actually was, never mind the Costa's nearby.

"Along the road dip shit! You really are fucked up mate!"

"Hang on Richard.."

"And stop calling me fucking Richard! Only my mother calls me that. You sound like your fucking Mrs!"

If only you knew..

I wanted to ask for the office address but thought better of it.

"Okay, see you there."

I opened the Sat Nav on Adam's mini, and to my relief Adam had programmed WORK into the menu. Selecting the address, I followed the guided instructions to Adam's workplace.

Adam worked at a large project management company in Bishops Stortford, who's offices were situated near to the high street. Assuming the nearest Costa coffee shop to the office was correct, I tentatively entered looking around for his friend. Hovering just short of the queue I looked around but could not see Richard there. Suddenly I felt a tug on the back of my trousers, pulling into Adam's crutch as Richard gave me an unwelcome 'wedgie' from behind.

"Alright numb nuts?" he said.

Looking round, I saw the familiar grin of Richard, "Get them in, I'll grab a seat."

"Er.. what do you want?" I said uncertainly.

Richard frowned, "Fucking hell, a fucking flat white as normal, a large one. And grab some sugars."

Richard went to a table in the corner of the café, while I purchased a skinny caffe latte and flat white for Richard. I took the drinks to the table and sat opposite Adam's friend.

"Cheers buddy," he grabbed the coffee, and poured two brown sugars into the cup, stirring it roughly. Staring at my drink he exclaimed, "What the fuck's that?"

"Skinny latte."

"Jesus! You gone off your macchiatos then? A bit girlie for you aint it?"

I faked a laugh, "Yeah, just fancied a change I guess. Evette likes them."

Slurping loudly from his cup, Richard stared at Adam before him. He was the total opposite of Adam, overweight, scruffily dressed, sporting a large un-groomed beard. His manner was coarse, and profanity was his preferred means of expression.

"So knob head, what's the problem then?"

I looked briefly into his eyes, then looked away, preferring to gaze around the café aimlessly.

Richard frowned, "What's up with you? You tell me to meet you here coz you can't go into the office, what have you finally shagged Cheryl then and can't face her?"

Who's Cheryl?

"No, nothing like that…" I did not want to ask the obvious question, but could not resist , almost knowing Richard's likely reply.

"Cheryl who?"

"Oh fuck off! What's up with you? You got dementia or something? Stop fucking about! Cheryl in the fucking office, that's who!" he barked.

"Oh yeah, that Cheryl. Sorry I am fucking about," I said, but suddenly in my mind Cheryl had become more important than my own situation.

Why would Richard say that? Is Adam having an affair?

I had to know, but how? I had to go into the Lion's den.

"So as I am here, we might as well go in."

"Where?"

"The office."

"You really are a fucking tart Ad's! I thought you said that you couldn't go in."

"So? Can't I change my mind?"

Richard shrugged, "Suppose so. But why didn't you want to

come in in the first instance?"

I knew that I would have to come up with some excuse, so why not the truth? Or at least some of it.

"Well to be honest, Evette has chucked me out."

"Fuck! Why is that?"

"She caught me shagging her best mate."

Richard unexpectedly burst out laughing.

"What? You? Shagged her best mate? Fuck me, you don't do things by halves do you."

I shook my head, "Not this time."

"Not any time," retorted Richard, "I thought you were Mr Monogamous."

I immediately felt happier to hear that reference to my husband.

"I thought so too, but I couldn't help myself. It kind of just happened"

"Where'd you shag her?"

"Does that matter?"

"Of course!"

"In our en-suite shower."

"Get in! Home fucking run!" laughed Richard, thoroughly enjoying the adventure.

"You don't have to sound so happy Richard! This is really fucked up!" I could feel tears start to well up in Adam's eyes. I turned away from Richard's gaze.

"Oh.. fuck.. sorry mate, I don't mean to take the piss."

I quickly collected myself, "Forget it. Can we just go to the office please?"

"In a minute mate, come on, tell me about it. I want to help really I do."

"You wouldn't believe this last couple of days Rich, even if I filmed it all," I said, wiping away the tears from Adam's eyes.

"So, tell me, how long have you been shagging her mate?"

"I haven't, it was purely a one off. Sort of an experiment at first if you like."

"Experiment? Tell me more," he grinned, then quickly pulled his face straight again, "Sorry.. go on."

"You don't need to know the details, but until Evette actually caught me with her friend, we had no problems that I was aware of."

"So you're getting plenty then?"

I struggled to answer that one. "Enough.. let's just say that."

"So why shag her mate?"

"Like I said, but was sorry of an experiment… just leave it at that please."

Richard shrugged, and after gulping down his coffee, he led the way to the office across the high street.

I had never been to Adam's work before, and had no real idea who anyone was, nor what they or even Adam actually did for a living. I would have to bluff my way through the day.

#

As soon as we entered the main office, I felt my courage weaken. The office was large and open plan with approximately 20 or so desks lined up on both sides, and a large board room / management office at the rear. As we walked through, several people greeted me, both male and female, to which I just nodded to each one. A curvy figured woman approached us as we walked to the far side of the room. She was in her mid 30's, petite build but with a large bosom barely contained beneath a tight-fitting white blouse. And I found myself staring directly at them! Such was the instinctive 'man lust' within Adam's body.

"Er eyes up, I have a face too you know." she said as she breezed past. I quickly looked directly into her eyes, which were glistening with mischief.

Bloody hell, I have been caught staring at a pair of tits!

"Ha haa…" whispered Richard, "Captured!"

Turning to speak to the woman as she passed, Richard said aloud, "Sorry Cheryl darling, he's a pervert don't you know."

"I wasn't talking to Adam Rich, but you! You pervert!"

"As if I would do that Cheryl, a true gentleman me."

Leaning close, he whispered into Adam's ear, "I would so fuck that!"

Me too, I thought briefly, then admonished Adam in my mind.

Fucking hell Adam! Wind it in a little please!

Richard led me to a large desk where several computer monitors were placed. One side was tidy, and uncluttered, the other a mess with numerous papers and files stacked untidily on the ends.

Unsurprisingly, Richard chose the messy side to my relief. On the opposite desk I saw a picture of myself, much to my liking.

Ahh thank you for thinking about me Adam..

I was still curious about Cheryl, and needed to know more about her. Taking a seat at Adam's desk, I leaned over towards Richard, "Have you ever?" I asked.

"Ever what?"

"You know, fucked Cheryl"

"Fuck off! I'd stand no chance, mind you if you and your Mrs are off, you definitely could."

"Me? Why's that?"

Richard looked slightly dumfounded, and frowned "You are fucked up mate, or fucking blind! She's been after you for fucking ages, you must know surely"

"I hadn't noticed"

"What? What's up with you? You *have* turned into your Mrs or you're turning queer!?"

I suddenly felt uncomfortable, was it that obvious?

"I don't know what you mean" I said.

"Has shagging your wife's mate fucked your brain up? Every drink, office do, she is all over you. Plus even every time you pass her on the stairs, or in the lifts she pushes her tits out at you."

He stared at my blank expression on Adam's face, "In fact, mate, she has a sign over her head saying, '*Please fuck the arse off me Adam'* that everyone else can see except you!"

"Yeah, but I have never done anything, have I?" I said, almost dreading Richard's next sentence.

"You haven't yet. Mind you after today you have gone up in my estimation. You might as well shag Cheryl too. I definitely fucking would!"

I gazed at the rear end of Cheryl as she gracefully walked from view. The thought of her naked suddenly flashed into my mind, and Adam's cock made an instant jolt in his underpants. *Fuck me... don't you start!* I quickly changed the subject to the work in hand.

"Let's get on with the project Rich, I am starting to feel unwell again."

"Oh, okay. Right I'll talk you through it."

After a short informal presentation of Richard's ideas, I stared aimlessly at his reports and slide shows on the screen. I had no real idea what Richard was talking about, nor did I care. Deep down, I knew that this visit would be futile but thought it may give a clue to Adam's whereabouts. He couldn't just disappear! I slowly scrolled through several documents as Richard's voice droned in the background, after which I told him all was fine.

"What, everything?" he said.

"Seems okay" I said with a hint of uncertainty.

"Fuck me, that's a first. Okay, I'll submit it then."

Taking my cue, I decided now would be a good time to depart.

"Right then, I'm off, I need to check if Evette's alright. See ya!"

Before Richard could answer, I jumped up and dashed from the office. A sudden flight impulse came over me with every step towards the exit. As my pace quickened with each stride, so did my emotions. Adams heart was racing as my panic increased, and I threw open the main office entrance door to escape, bursting through, right into the soft voluptuous body of Cheryl! I could not stop in time, and we collided, knocking Cheryl back a few steps causing her to drop a pile of papers she was carrying.

"Oh my God Adam!" she yelled, as she staggered to stay upright. I could not say anything, and the sound of cheers and laughter from inside the office did not help as a few people nearby noticed the incident, including Richard.

"Oh Fuck me! His wife gives him the elbow, and he's jumped straight on top of Cheryl! Get a room mate at least!" he shouted, laughing loudly for all to hear.

I was like a rabbit caught in the headlights and I looked for an escape. Seeing the toilet doors to the office I dashed inside, but instinctively chose the ladies toilets as my place of refuge.

Once inside, I struggled to breath as panic overtook me. I could hear Cheryl's voice calling out Adam's name, but this only made matters worse. Seeking further sanctuary, I dived into the nearest cubicle, locked the door and sat on the toilet seat, hugging Adam's knees to his chest. My mind was a whirl, it seemed that everything had abruptly come to a head.

I can't cope..

The situation was too much. I was trapped in my husband's body with no way out. I have lost him, lost my best friend, my mother, and my own self all in one short day. Now I am trapped sitting on a toilet seat with an unknown rival, slimmer, sexier, and probably younger than me, stalking outside, undoubtedly waiting to pounce on my husband. I then did the only thing I could do, burst into floods of tears.

As I sobbed, I became aware of the entrance door opening, and the footsteps of a person outside the cubical. Although it was me who was actually crying, I was more aware of the loud cries of Adam as I sobbed, which made matters in my mind worse. I had never heard him cry in that way, and although I supposedly had control, I could not make him stop. It was a perpetual spiral of fear and despair.

"Adam, Adam.. are you alright?" said Cheryl, her voice was soft and caring, echoing lightly in the room. I tried hard to contain myself but I still could not hold in my emotions.

"No.." I whined, "I'm lost."

"Open the door Adam, you can't stay in here."

"I can, please just leave me alone. I'll be alright in a few minutes."

"No you can't stay here Adam. This is the ladies toilets"

I could not answer, but just wailed out loud instead. The noise of Adam's crying now echoing loudly throughout the space. Another voice resounded outside harshly, "What's he up too? Get him out, I want to use the loo!"

There followed several loud bangs on the cubical door, as another woman sought use of the toilets.

"Get out! This is the ladies toilet!" she yelled.

"I can't! Go away!" I yelled, "Use another toilet!"

The voice outside was undeterred, "Right, I'm calling the management!" she exclaimed, and her heavy footsteps sounded her retreat. I could hear the voice of Cheryl trying to appease the woman, and several voices of men outside the toilets apparently enjoying the drama. The door outside appeared to close, and the voices diminished, giving me some respite. I knew that I could not stay there any longer and stood and slowly opened the catch pulling the door partially ajar.

As I stepped from the cubicle, Cheryl walked back in, closing the door behind her. I tried to walk past without explanation, but she stopped me with a gently placed hand on Adam's chest.

"Adam," she said softly. "What on earth is wrong?"

I could not say anything but looked her in the eyes. Cheryl could see the pain in the blue eyes of Adam, now reddened though the tears. I felt his face was trembling as my emotions began to crescendo again.

"I can't tell you .."

Adam's lips trembled as I looked into the warm eyes of Cheryl. I needed comfort, and found myself surrendering to a warm and welcome embrace as Cheryl hugged Adam close. I laid Adam's head into Cheryl's shoulder, and unleashed further sobs as she stroked Adam's hair.

"Hush hush, it's alright , it's going to be alright Adam. Whatever it is."

I felt comfort for the first time that day, real comfort . Although my instincts were to pull away from this woman, Adam's body was comforted by it. He longed for it, and so did I. Although I craved and enjoyed the emotional comfort of Cheryl's embrace, I could feel Adam's body getting aroused. I could feel every curve of Cheryl's body, in particular her large firm breasts which seemed to have a power of their own. Her hips were pressed gently against Adam's groin, and I could feel his erection beginning to build. I wanted to pull away instinctively, but the pleasure of the embrace, the smell of Cheryl's perfume, and the feel of her body against his took over.

We embraced for a minute, and as my emotions calmed I lifted Adam's head from Cheryl's shoulder and gazed into her eyes. An overwhelming urge to kiss Cheryl flooded over me, until the sudden entrance of the angry woman interrupted us.

"Oh charming! If you don't mind I wish to use the convenience !"

"Sorry," said Cheryl , "we are going now."

Cheryl led me out of the toilet and down though the hallway to the office lifts.

"Let's go for a drink, or get some air," she said, "maybe if you want you can tell me what's wrong."

I needed a friend and despite my early impression of Cheryl being a sexual predator, I could now only see the concern of a friend in her eyes. A very attractive and sexy friend.

I followed Cheryl willingly.

But where would this now lead…

12

SHE'S A COMPLETE FUCKING BITCH

Cheryl and I walked silently from the building away from the busy shops, in the direction of the central town park. After a short dash across the road to avoid the busy afternoon traffic, we walked into the park and then along a path next to the river where a pop-up cycle coffee bar was situated. The sun was shining, and the warmth of the hot sun rays calmed me. I was more than happy to be guided by this attractive stranger.

"Do you want a coffee Adam? Or shall we just walk along the river and talk?"

I am not a huge coffee drinker, and the suggestion of an aimless walk sounded more attractive.

"We can walk, if you don't mind. I need to clear my head."

Cheryl smiled, "Okay, come on, let's see if we can cheer you up." She suddenly slipped her arm through Adam's and pulled his body close as we walked on. For a brief moment I was surprised, but Cheryl's contact felt more as a genuine friend than one of a sexual diva. I felt relaxed and happy, walking arm in arm with her, enjoying her support.

After a short period Cheryl spoke, "So Adam, do you want to tell me what's happening? I have never seen you like that, and I am worried."

I hesitated, although Cheryl knew Adam, I had no idea what their relationship was. Were they close friends? Were they just colleagues? Had Adam ever spoken to her about his relationship before?

What does she know?

"It's a long story," I said.

"We have time, I don't have to be back this afternoon, other than to get my bag, so we have as long as you want really."

I did not reply. I was confused by Cheryl. To me she was a complete stranger, but to Adam she was obviously very attractive as our embrace in the toilets had clearly shown. To be frank, I did not really know what I wanted from Cheryl. My intention of going to Adam's work was to find possible answers on how to regain my life and leave Adam's body. Yet on the other hand I was intrigued to discover Adam's life away from me. Was he faithful? Did he still love me? Cheryl might be able to re-assure me and help me understand Adam better.

The answer must lie in Adam, but I was unable to reach him in any way. Nor could I find Dr Sahasrabudhhe. That's if he had ever existed in the first place. Cheryl at this time was my only potential clue in finding Adam.

She suddenly stopped walking, and gently pulled me to a halt by a bench. "Adam, do you want to talk? We can sit here."

I nodded, and we sat close together with Cheryl taking Adam's hand. "Richard told me that you and your wife have split up. Is that why you were crying?"

"Yes, but it's much more than that."

"You can tell me, I know we are not great friends and that, but we always talk. And you've said that you have had problems before."

I was suddenly annoyed, *'He's been slagging me off to her!'* I withdrew Adam's hand suddenly.

"What did he.. " I quickly corrected myself. "Er.. I tell you? I can't remember exactly."

"Well, mainly that you and she were having problems over a baby."

My anger quickly rose, "In what way?" I said sharply.

Cheryl became obviously uncomfortable with the tone coming from Adam, "Well, I can't exactly remember the details Adam."

"You must do."

"Why would I? In fact you told *me* Adam. Surely you must remember what you said?"

I turned away, "I'm just not myself today. My mind isn't right, I just can't think or remember anything."

Cheryl placed a hand on Adam's back, then slowly ran her palm over to his shoulder, pulling his body close to her in a half embrace. "I can see that, something terrible must have happened. This isn't like you at all. Please Adam tell me what happened. You can trust me. I promise that I won't say anything to anybody."

I felt my anger wane and I settled Adam's head into Cheryl's shoulder.

"If I tell you, promise me you won't laugh or tell anyone else please. Promise me."

"I won't, I promise."

I was desperate to talk to anyone, but also to maybe get another girl's view of her and Adam's relationship.

Maybe this is fate guiding me, maybe Cheryl is holding the key.

"It all started a few months ago when we began trying for a baby. I.. that is we were unable to conceive, which meant we had to try a more scientific approach. Checking basal temperatures, ovulation charts, and that. Then Adam… " I hesitated, *'Get a grip Eve! You're Adam now!'*

"…Then I began to do weird things.."

"Weird things?" said Cheryl, "Nothing too weird I hope.."

I shook Adam's head, "I don't think so, but I did start, well… masturbating.."

Cheryl raised her eyebrows, "Masturbating? Really ? That isn't weird Adam. Everybody does that."

"Yes, but I was doing it in bed, when Evette was sleeping."

"Why didn't you just wake her up and make love properly?"

"I can't… we can't just do that. Because we are trying for the baby."

Cheryl laughed lightly, "Adam, just because you are trying for a baby doesn't mean you can't make love normally."

"But we can only do it when Evette is at her most fertile, or there's no point to it!"

"Oh my God Adam, there is more to sex than just getting pregnant!"

"Not if we really want a baby, otherwise we are just wasting semen."

Cheryl pulled away and faced me.

"Is that your or your wife's view Adam?" she said firmly.

"Our view, both of us."

She paused, "Then, why do you feel the need to masturbate when she is sleeping Adam?"

I had no answer, *'It's time for the truth Evette.'*

"To be honest, it's Evette's idea. She doesn't want sex unless we are trying for the baby."

"Oh Adam, that's wrong. You need to tell her."

"But how do you know that's wrong? You haven't had children. Have you?"

"It's not about children Adam. Sex is a part of your relationship, it should be wonderful, and loving. Not clinical. You might as well just wank into a test tube and squirt it up there!"

'That's what Adam said..' I thought.

"But I think it's me. I am becoming more demanding, asking for sex all the time. I walk behind Evette's back and grab her boobs. I waggle a lot; my cock has a hard on half the time. It must be me, not her!"

"Does she like you grabbing her boobs?"

"No, she shouts at me, even if I look at them."

"What? But you're married."

"Why should that matter? She is entitled to her privacy."

Cheryl appeared amused, "Really Adam? This isn't the Victorian times. It's modern day."

"No you don't get it. I spend half my time staring at her boobs, I grab her bum, I get horny just washing myself in the shower. There's definitely something wrong with me."

"There isn't, believe me. You are no different to any man I know."

"But I am obsessed with boobs, I even looked at yours!"

Cheryl laughed, "Well that's honesty I suppose, but too be honest I haven't ever noticed you doing that. So at least you are discrete." She playfully touched Adam's nose. I was not convinced though.

"You have it wrong. I'm a pervert, I must be."

"Adam, I am sure you are not."

"How would you know?"

"You do not seem anything like that to me Adam."

"That's not what everyone thinks though is it?"

"I don't know of one person who thinks that of you Adam. Not one."

"I do.."

"Who Adam?"

"Evette, she does, and she knows me better than anyone."

"This is ridiculous Adam, frankly, from what you have told me you have not done anything wrong. If your wife treated you normally, I am sure you would not have masturbated in the bed."

Cheryl was quickly beginning to annoy me now.

'What do you bloody know?'

I now felt that I had to defend myself.

"Well, she thinks she is normal, and I am abnormal." I protested.

"Well she is a complete fucking bitch!"

'You don't even know me! .. Bitch!'

In an instant, my original suspicions of Cheryl returned, and my anger and jealousy quickly grew. I sat bolt upright to face Cheryl and interrogated her.

"Have you … have *we* I mean, ever had an affair?" I demanded.

"What?"

"Have we ever had an affair? Richard seems to think so!"

"I'm sorry Adam, but why are you saying that? Surely you would know that!"

I stood abruptly, hands on Adam's hips, "So we have!"

"What? I don't understand?"

I was now convinced, and shouted at her, "That's a yes then! You have been having an affair with my … my… my body!"

Cheryl too stood and faced Adam angrily, "What are you going on about Adam?"

"You! Me! Having an affair!"

"Look, I think you're confused."

"You're not exactly denying it! Are you?"

"But.."

"ARE YOU CHERYL?" Adams voice and demeanour were aggressive.

Cheryl quickly turned and marched away furiously. "Get some fucking help Adam!"

I was now incensed, "Yeah ! Walk away! You tart!"

'Fucking bitch, who does she think she's kidding. She's definitely shagging him!

I didn't know what to do, so I walked slowly behind the ever vanishing Cheryl in the general direction of Adam's car.

There was no point in hanging around further. Seeing her and Richard had proven fruitless other than confirming in my mind that Cheryl and Adam were lovers. The one thing I had managed to do is thoroughly isolate myself further. How could I carry on as Adam now? How could I face his workmates after my outburst in the toilets? I would just have to return home and try and patch things up with my other self.

Arriving at Adam's car, I searched his pockets for the car keys, but to my horror I had lost them. I was not used to keeping items in pockets and must have placed them down somewhere. I quickly rushed to the coffee shop, only to be told that no one had handed any in. There was only one other place, Adam's office. I searched for his phone to call Richard, but that was missing too.

'Shit! I must have left them in the office!'

I had no choice but to return to Adam's office. Hopefully Cheryl would have gone, and I would ignore Richard and just walk out.

'I'll just simply walk in and leave ... nothing will go wrong ...

Taking a few deep breaths, I walked bristly to the office building.

#

Inside Adam's work, Cheryl was now in tears, and being comforted by Michael, the Director of the company in the board room. She had explained what had happened and what Adam had said, despite her promise to me. She had not gone into any detail but had told Michael of her concern for Adam's welfare, and that he may need professional help. At the time, Michael was looking through the glass office boardroom windows when he saw me as Adam appear at the office entrance door.

"He's here Cheryl, I am just going to have a word."

#

I took a deep breath as I entered the office, Richard was not at his desk, so I walked briskly to Adam's desk where I was pleased to see his phone and the car keys next to the computer. *'Thank God.'*

A deep voice behind me suddenly spoke out, startling me.

"A word please Adam?"

I looked around to see Michael standing behind me, and behind him peering through the office glass was Cheryl. I had met Michael previously, but I could not remember his name, or what his position was. I stared at Cheryl through the glass intently, *'Fucking bitch! She's told him everything!'*

"I'm sorry, but I only came back for my phone, I'm not feeling well." I said, and I tried to turn away, but Michael placed a hand firmly on Adam's arm. I looked at him directly. He was a large man in his forties, well built, and a strong jawline. His eyes narrowed angrily, and I felt threatened.

"Sorry Adam, but I think you should come with me." he said, holding Adam's arm in a strong grip.

"What has she told you?" I said , in a surprising to me, emotion of aggression. I could feel Adam's testosterone swelling up as the adrenaline flooded into his body.

"She hasn't said anything, we just need to talk in private," said Michael firmly, "we don't want to embarrass anybody here do we."

I looked around me at the many faces looking on around the office. This was not what I had planned at all. My anger rose alarmingly, and I shouted across at Cheryl. "What have you told him you fucking nosey bitch?"

"Now calm down Adam!" said Michael.

"Calm down? I am fucking calm!"

In truth, I could barely control myself. I was not used to male aggression, and though usually I was a complete wimp, in Adam's body I felt huge.

"Did she tell you she's been shagging my husband? Did she? Fucking Tart!"

"What are you talking about?" said Michael bemused, "she's said no such thing!"

"Don't lie!" I yelled, "Do you think you're clever shagging my husband? Did you think I wouldn't find out? Tart!"

Richard stood nearby, and was considering intervening, but the entertainment was proving too much.

"Husband? Fuck me.. that's it! You've turned fucking queer!" he laughed, causing a ripple of chuckles from around.

Michael had heard enough, "Right Adam, get out!" he said aggressively, and tried to man handle me from the building. To my horror, I found myself striking out at Michael, punching him hard in the face knocking him to the floor. I stood above him, I could feel Adam's muscles were tense and bulging as I loomed threateningly over Michael.

Instead of me being my usual nervous wreck when it comes to any confrontation, I felt oddly amazing. Even though the thought of violence usually would horrify me, I felt empowerment and almost enjoyment from the experience.

Michael was not hurt by the blow , but surprised. He regained composure, and simply said, “You’re fired. Get out!”

I grabbed the phone and keys, and marched out ignoring everyone in the room, including Richard who attempted to follow me out. But a well-timed slam of the door as I departed thwarted his efforts to follow.

Outside though, once back at the car I paused and realised the enormity of what I had done. In one swift move I had ruined Adam’s career, embarrassed him in front of his entire office, and shunned what may be his closest friends. Everything he and I had built was now gone. I have lost myself, Adam and everyone who meant anything to me in one day.

Could life get any worse..

13

HELP HELP! RAPE RAPE!

Driving home I could not contain my sobbing and had to stop the car several times as the tears filled Adam's eyes. There was now only one place I could go, and one person I had to face. My other self.

Without the help of anyone, I was certain that I could never return to my normal self and find Adam. I thought of ringing her, but the idea was too weird to contemplate , and so far I had little success in communicating with her as Adam.

When I finally drove into our road, I was relieved to see my own car parked on the drive. I pulled up but paused to gather my thoughts.

'*How can I do this? Where do I begin?*

The only thing I could think of was trying to see if my other self remembered anything about the past couple of days, in particular the visit to 'The Rivers hospital' and Dr Sahasrabudhhe.

Armed with half a plan, I strode from the car to the front door. Placing the key in the door lock, I tired to turn it several times, but it failed to engage and unlock.

'Oh my God, she's changed the fucking locks already!'

I rang the doorbell, which after a few seconds crackled as my other self answered over the speaker.

"What do you want Adam?"

"I want to come in, have you changed the bloody locks already?"

"You can't come in; I have nothing to say to you."

One thing I knew about me, and her was how to press her anger buttons, so with a quick, "Okay, I'll go round to Mel's then," I stepped back just out of view of the doorbell and waited. As I predicted, after a few seconds the door was unlocked from within, and my other self threw back the door to rant at her fleeing husband.

"Go on then Adam, go back to that…"

Before she could react, using Adam's speed and strength I dived from cover and pushed past her and triumphantly claimed the hallway. I pushed her forwards onto the doorstep and partially closed the door, shutting the now screaming Evette outside.

"What? Adam! Open the door.. Now!" She pushed against the door in vain but could not overcome Adam's superior strength and weight.

"Not until you calm down and you agree to talk Evette." I said, giggling quietly at my neat trick.

"I have nothing to say to you Adam."

"Well, I am not going anywhere, and you're not coming in until we talk."

I turned and sat against the door as my other self ranted and raved outside, banging her fist on the door. Looking above , I realised that the lock had not been changed, but she had left the key in the lock blocking the mechanism from being opened from outside.

The door began to become uncomfortable against Adam's back as Evette continued to pound against it. I then stood and partially opened the door, but held it closed against her for a few more seconds as she pushed hard against it.

"I'm.. stronger … than … you … think… Adam!" she growled as she inched the door open. Amused at her efforts , I thought the best and most amusing thing would be to let her in. Abruptly!

Grinning in anticipation I suddenly stood away from the door, which flew open immediately as my other self, entered comically , screaming like an angry cat as she fell through the doorway. She stumbled into the middle of the hallway, just managing to catch herself before she fell. She turned angrily to face a now giggling Adam before her.

"Owww! You stupid bastard!" she screamed, "I could have broken my wrists."

"Well, you shouldn't have locked me out should you!"

"Well you shouldn't have pushed through the door!"

"Well you shouldn't have tried to push back in!"

"Well YOU shouldn't have shagged my fucking best friend!"

I did not have a reply but stood there looking sheepish. "Look I am sorry Evette, but you need to hear my side first."

She pulled a superior smug expression, *'God I pull some ugly faces sometimes..'* I thought, as she continued to rant at me.

"What could you possibly say that would excuse what you did? You shagged my best friend! My BEST friend Adam!"

"I know!"

"SO! You ADMIT IT!" she yelled angrily.

"I can hardly fucking deny it Evette! You caught us in the fucking act!"

"Well, you could at least try and make some excuse Adam!"

"What? Why? Would it make any difference?"

"No, but at least you could pretend to be sorry. Rather than just admit it!"

I stared at her, and could feel anger growing in Adam's body, "God I really did not realise that I am such a thick bitch!" I said clumsily.

"What? Are you calling me a thick bitch?"

"Yes, well, not just you. Us!"

Evette suddenly turned and marched into the kitchen, "I'm calling the police if you don't get out Adam!"

"No! This is my fucking home Evette!"

I followed her into the kitchen and saw her grabbing her iPhone from the charger. In a swift movement I grabbed her by the wrist and pulled the phone away. In seconds I felt a hard slap across Adam's face, followed by a sharp kick in the shins.

"Ow! For fuck sake Evette!" I yelled.

"Don't you swear at me," she yelled as she rained slap after slap at Adam's head and shoulders. I could not take any more, and using Adam's strength, I grabbed her in a bear hug, and lifting her off of the floor I sat her onto one of our kitchen swivel stools. Quickly looking around me as she screamed and shouted for help at the top of her voice, I pinned her wrists together with one hand and grabbed a nearby roll of clingfilm. Holding the end in my fingers as I held her wrists, I rapidly began to wrap the clingfilm around the screaming Evette, whilst spinning the chair round and around. To my amazement it actually worked! But it did little to silence the screams and profanity that my other self was now making, as she went through the alphabet of swear words and insults. *'Christ! I never knew I used that word!'* I thought when she got to the letter 'C'.

For a moment I contemplated wrapping the clingfilm around my victims mouth but I thought better of it, and stopped there.

"Right Evette, can we now speak?"

"Fuck you Adam!"

"Okay, you leave me no choice!" I then pulled a length of clingfilm from the rest of the roll and held it towards her face. She recoiled and acquiesced , "Okay, okay Adam. You win."

"Good, that's better."

"But mother is on her way, I just rang her before you arrived, so you had better untie me."

I knew that she would probably be lying but I thought I should check her phone just in case. Grabbing the iPhone, I tried to open it but due to fingerprint I.D it would not open it.

"Ha!" said my other self triumphantly, "can't open it Adam?"

With a smug smile, I calmly typed the PIN number in the phone and opened the call list.

"How do you know my pin Adam? That's private!"

"If only you knew Evette."

I examined the calls. "I see you called your mother numerous times, but strangely enough you don't seem to have got through."

She self looked away from me sheepishly.

"She won't answer me, I don't know why."

'I do' I thought, recalling her mother's attempt to 'breast feed' me earlier that day. I shuddered at the memory.

"Look, if you agree to talk Evette, I will untie you."

"NO! You untie me now, and then we will talk."

"No Evette, I know you too well, you will just kick off again."

"Oh fuck off Adam! HELP HELP ! RAPE RAPE!!" she screamed.

'Fucking Bitch!"

"Right! If you're going to act like a child, I will treat you like one!" I grabbed hold of her shoulders and began to spin the chair round and round as she continued to scream louder and longer.

"Are you going to shut up?"

"NO!"

Undeterred bye her hysterics, I span her faster and harder until the chair began rocking, almost falling over as Adam's strong arms whirled her around and around.

"I'm going to be sick. Stop, Adam please STOP!"

"Are you going to talk?"

"YES YES! " she screamed, to which I grabbed her shoulders

bringing the chair to a halt. To my surprise though, she burst into floods of tears. It was an odd sensation , seeing one's self from a distance. Even though I was looking at her almost as an enemy, I realised that she was also a victim of this bizarre circumstance. She too had lost everything, her husband, her mother, her best friend. We needed to work together, so I had to get her on my side. I slung my arms around her and hugged my other self closely, as I too began to cry. There followed a flooding of tearful apologies as I held my other self tightly, both of us sobbing as the pent up frustrations were released from both our bodies.

I stood upright; and Adam's hand instinctively stroked her cheek wiping away the tears. "Look, I am going to untie you, and if you want to run or call the police do so. But all I want to do is talk. I need to tell you exactly what has happened. If you'll let me."

"Okay, I promise."

I quickly pulled the clingfilm away from her and returned her phone. I then turned and walked to the wine rack, and opened a bottle of Red and poured out two large goblets, handing one to my other self. Both of us took large swigs of the wine, exactly mimicking each other's habits.

"That's good," we both said in unison.

We walked into the lounge and sat opposite each other. I began, "Look first of all before you say anything, can you just listen to what I have to tell you, and keep an open mind. Can you do that?"

"Yes, if you promise to tell me how long you and Mel have been shagging."

"I will tell you everything, including what happened between Mel and me. But first I want to talk about the other day."

"What other day? When we rowed over sex? Is that why you shagged her?"

"No, no.. I will get to all that later. You went to see that Doctor."

"Katrina? Yes I saw her."

"No, the one at The Rivers, Doctor Sahasrabudhhe. The Indian doctor."

"I'm not sure."

"What do you mean you're not sure? Did you go or not?"

"It's none of your business Adam!"

"It is!"

"No it's not.. oh this is useless, you think you can rule me don't you?"

"No!"

"You think that you own me!"

"What the fuck are you on about Evette?"

"Just because I went to see a doctor, about YOU by the way because of your perverted ways, you think it's your business!"

"It *IS* my fucking business Evette!" I shouted angrily.

"No! If I did go and see the doctor, it has nothing to do with you."

"He shagged you, didn't he? That Doctor."

My other self was taken aback, and she stared at me for a few moments. "What has Mel said?"

I thought it was time to explain.. if I can.

"Not Mel, me! I told me."

She frowned at me, "You're not making sense Adam."

"Just listen Evette, I tried to tell you this morning. Something weird has happened after you, well, we to be accurate, saw that doctor. Part of your body, or soul, or spirit, call it what you like, came into me. Well into Adam's body to be precise."

"Oh don't start that again Adam," she said crossly.

"It is true! I.. well you.. are in me!"

"Right, I've had enough of this. I'm going!" she snapped and stood to try and push past me and leave. Feeling the adrenalin and anger rising into Adam's body, I grabbed her by each wrist, shaking them angrily.

"Why the fuck would I make something like that up?" I yelled, now exasperated. "Why Evette? WHY???"

My other self shook in fear as her husband bellowed at her aggressively. I looked into her eyes and saw the fear and weakness in her. I stopped shouting, and slowly released her wrists.

'*This isn't the way! What am I doing?*' I thought.

"Look Evette, I am sorry for shouting, but you have to listen. I know it's unbelievable, but please just hear me out. I will tell you exactly what happened to you, blow by blow. Word by word. If I am wrong, and it's different than you remember, then maybe I am having a mental breakdown, and you can stick me in hospital or something. Okay?"

To my surprise, and relief, she nodded. I could see that deep down, she knew that something strange had occurred when she had visited Dr Sahasrabudhhe, but as in my mind she probably believed that she must have had some kind of vivid dream in Mel's car.

I calmly retold the whole Dr Sahasrabudhhe visit to my other self, recounting each word spoken by the doctor, what he looked like, how handsome he was, about the tea he gave her, the garden, the music, and lastly how he apparently seduced her.

With each sentence I could see her eyes widening and her mouth dropping in disbelief. In particular when I mentioned her masturbating in Mel's Figaro.

"You see Evette, he has somehow put part of you, well of us to be precise, into Adam. But the hardest thing is, I don't know where Adam is right now."

"Fuck ..." she said and took a large drink. "I thought I must have somehow dreamt the whole thing."

"Imagine how I bloody feel!" I said downing my own glass of wine.

I could see her pondering the whole absurd situation over and over on her head. She placed her glass down and held both her hands on her temples rubbing them slightly.

"But.. what I don't get Adam, if you, or me or whatever is inside you, how am I still here? I thought this body swap thing was just that, so you should be in me."

"I don't know, that's why we need to find that doctor."

We spoke on, telling each other about our day, about our independent visits to our mother, how I first discovered that I was now a man and what that was like. The experience of having a cock, shagging Mel, Cheryl, the fight at Adam's work, everything.

With each minute that past, my other self gradually seemed to grasp and accept what I as Adam, was saying, and she seemed to see more and more of her own being inside Adam's body. We spoke of what it was like being Adam, how our own personality differed from within each body's point of view. The more we spoke, the more we both understood him, now all we needed to do was find him.

But first we needed to find Doctor Sahasrabudhhe..

14

SEEKING DR SAHASABUDDHE

Our first port of call was The Rivers hospital. I drove us both there in Adam's car, parking it near to the building site as before. We walked into the reception where we were greeted by a smart looking receptionist.

"Can I help you?" she said with a well-rehearsed smile.

We both answered immediately, both of us being used to taking control in these situations. "Yes," we said in exact unison.

Recognising my other self's usual role of taking control when her and Adam were together, I allowed her the lead to avoid confusion.

"You explain Evette."

"We are here to see Doctor Sahasrabudhhe, is he available please?"

The receptionist appeared slightly confused and began to type the name onto her computer. "Doctor ? How do you spell that please?"

We looked at each other briefly and shrugged. "Do you still have the card?" I said.

"No, Melisa tore it up I think."

"What was the reason for you wanting to see him?" said the receptionist.

"It's private."

"I understand that, but can you tell me what field of expertise he was a specialist in? Maybe he is a visiting practitioner or new perhaps."

"The card said that he was a sexual therapist."

"I am afraid that we do not cater for that here."

I then intervened, "Look, we came here a few days ago, we had a card with this address on. We came here and I, well my wife saw this man. It was in an office near where the building work is being done."

"Sorry Sir, but that it's impossible. That area is being refurbished, no procedure or visits are being undertaken there until the construction is completed."

"So who did we see?"

"I do not know sir, maybe you went to a different hospital."

I looked at Evette expecting a huge outburst, but instead I saw the same confused dejected and lost expression as I felt.

"Let's go to where Mel parked the car.. maybe , just maybe the card will still be there." I suggested.

We walked from the reception over to the car park area where the construction site was still active. Searching amongst the mud, grass and dirt around the floor failed to find any trace of the card. All seemed to be lost. Walking back to the car, we barely had a word to say to each other. Our deepest thoughts were not that they could find no trace of the doctor, but more that they could not find or possibly find out where Adam had gone.

We drove back from the hospital in silence, both in deep thought. I was trying hard to think of how I could maybe find Doctor Sahasrabudhhe, and free me from Adam's body. But unbeknown to me at the time, my other self began to arrive at a different conclusion. I made the odd suggestion as to a plan of action but received no more than a casual grunt in reply. The silence was beginning to get to me and sensing something was wrong I tried to gain some response from her.

"What about seeing Katrina?"

"Seeing her about what, Adam?"

"Well, she may have given us the card in the first place?"

"I don't think there ever was a card Adam." she said flatly. "In fact, I think that this is all your doing."

I was stunned momentarily, "What? How can you say that?"

"Well Adam, until a couple of hours ago, I thought this doctor thing was just a dream I had. But then you told me this frankly questionable tale about you, well me, being in your body Adam, making you behave weirdly. But now I realise that the real reason that you are acting oddly Adam, is the fact that YOU shagged my best friend, and YOU are trying to get me to think that I am going mad."

I brought the car to an abrupt halt in the middle of the road, causing a cacophony of horns and verbal abuse from the cars and drivers behind me.

"What are you doing Adam?"

"I can't believe you. Earlier you agreed that we had swapped bodies, you believed me!"

"No.. Adam!"

"You did!"

"No.. Adam! I did not believe ; you have just tricked me into believing . This whole thing has been some sort of a stunt! A sick attempt to brainwash me, simply because you were unfaithful!"

"I don't fucking believe you!" I said, exasperated.

"Well .. Adam!" she replied, with extra emphasis on Adam's name, "that alone proves that you are not me. Because if you indeed were me, you would not be so stupid as to think that I would fall for such a nasty trick."

The cars behind by now were trying to edge past Adam's car, and the drivers from both directions were honking their horns furiously, and shouting.

"Just drive Adam! Before you cause an accident."

"But Evette!"

"DRIVE ADAM ! JUST FUCKING DRIVE!" screamed Evette hysterically.

Now fully flustered and aghast at her change of heart, I rammed the car into gear and booted the accelerator hard causing it to leap forward abruptly. I was glaring at my other self, and not at the road, as we moved forward. She began screaming incoherently in the passenger seat, but I could not understand what she was saying due to the intense stress of the situation, until a sickening crunch of metal brought me back to my senses.

"Oh that's fucking great Adam! Now look what you have done."

Without realising the traffic ahead was moving slowly I had collided with the car in front. The impact was low, due to the fact that I had barely driven a few feet, but the damage had been done. I bashed the steering wheel in frustration with both hands.

"Fuck, fuck .. FUCK FUCK FUCK!!!"

Evette too was in full flight, screaming at me, blaming me for everything. Reciting each moment of the past 24 hours in a torrent of hysterical, rapid indecipherable sentences. I too was trying to retort but I struggled to get a word over her. So intent on arguing were we, I failed to notice the driver of the car I had crashed into was standing at the door. He tried to get some response, but neither of us would even acknowledge his presence.

"Excuse me, you have hit my car.." he said, but on getting no reaction, he walked forward and took a number of photographs on his phone as we screamed at each other.

"Can I have you name and address please?" he said politely. I was aware of his request, but could only respond in a way that Adam's body allowed. In a furious loud testosterone enthused bellow.

"FUCK THE FUCK OFF! MATE. OKAY?"

The poor driver backed away from the door and stood there slightly stunned for a moment. Seeing no point of engaging any conversation from the raging pair before him, and the ever growing sounding of car horns around him, he decide retreat was the order of the moment. He fumbled in his pocket before throwing a card into the open window of our car.

"Here's my details," he said, but on receiving no response, he quickly returned to his own car and drove away.

I breathed in and out slowly, with Adams eye's closed and steadily I regained some composure. Choosing not to inspect the damage to Adam's car, and to ignore the other rebuking horns from the queue behind I began to drive forwards as the traffic started to move freely. My mind was a turmoil following the sudden back lash of my other self, but I could not think about it and drive. I had no idea how this was going to end as we both sat in silence for the rest of the journey, but it soon became clear when we arrived at our home where Evette stood. With barely a sidewards glance and a curt, "Goodbye Adam," she rushed from the car into our home and slammed the door.

As I watched her go, I realised that she was not me, and I not her. Although I thought we were the same person, I am not like her. I cannot be that unreasonable, hard hearted, cold and unloving woman. I am not like her. I am me, and she… she is someone else. What if it *is* me who is mad, and I am really Adam and my mind has somehow been damaged? Whoever I may be, I am not like that woman. She is Evette, and I do not want to be her.

I stepped out of the car and examined the damage from the accident. There was hardly anything other than a slight scuff, which was a small mercy ending to an appalling day.

I decided to drive to calm my mind and give Evette time alone. At the very least I felt that between us, there would be some sort of resolution as I could not see her just leaving things as they were. I would return later, but a drink was needed. '*A big fucking drink!*

15

THAT'S NOT COKE IS IT?

After a short drive to clear my mind, I stopped the car at a nearby nature park. I layed the seat partially back, and I closed Adam's eyes for a few seconds, allowing my mind to rest. I knew that ringing Evette would be futile, and my phone call would almost certainly be ignored.

I decided to check the phone to see if she had maybe sent a text , or had tried to ring me. I opened Adam's phone and began to scroll through the many apps. It had not actually occurred to me to explore his phone initially because I thought that Adam would use access codes, but it was soon evident that he had initiated fingerprint recognition, so he now had no secrets from me.

I quickly read through his Facebook page, messenger and a few WhatsApp groups that he and his friends belonged to. But it displayed little that I did not already know about him, apart from the fact that when texting his friends he swore far more often than in my company. Adam had many friends and contacts, but he made few phone calls. I looked for Cheryl in his contacts, who for a while I was certain had a relationship with him, but she was completely missing from his phone. There were no dating apps, no private memberships to porn sites, in fact there was nothing untoward in his diary, text messages or history that gave any hint of an unhappy or dissatisfied partner.

'Why had I misjudged him so?'

I laughed at the many photographs he had stored of us both. The videos of our holidays together though made me sad when I heard his voice talking and laughing. In Adam's head when I spoke his voice was different, but hearing him on the video deepened my sadness and longing for my old life and own identity back. Again, I began sobbing, and dropped the phone onto Adam's lap.

As I wept, a faint voice disturbed my cries. "Hello? Hello? Ad's? Is that you?"

The voice was coming from Adam's phone, which was now

displaying the name 'Tomo' on the face. I had heard Adam mention the name before as someone that he played football with at his gym. I put the phone onto the speaker.

"Hello?" I said, slightly hesitantly.

"Hello mate, what do I owe the honour?" the voice replied.

I paused, slightly confused as to who made the call, "I thought you called me?"

"Fuck did I mate, why the fuck do I want to talk to you?" the voice had an Australian type accent and he replied in a mocking friendly fashion.

"Sorry, I think I accidentally finger phoned you."

"What? Fucking pervert! You wish you fucking fingered me!" the voice laughed loudly, "So what have you been up too? I've not seen you for a while."

I had no idea again of most of Adam's relationships, so I could not instigate much of a conversation, but I felt an overwhelming need to speak to someone, anyone…

'A small bit of honesty might help here,'

"Not much to be honest," I said, "in fact I am pretty fucked up right now."

"Why? What's happened mate?"

"It's a very long story , but basically I have had a sort of… weird mental illness, and I have lost part of my memory."

"Fuck! Have you had a stroke or something?"

"Well, the doctors don't really know but basically they're still testing. I just find it hard to remember stuff occasionally."

"Fuck… what are you doing now then?"

"Now? I'm currently trying not to split up from my partner."

"What? Has she dumped you mate?"

"I think so, we've been arguing a lot and she's basically chucked me out?"

"Seems a bit harsh when you've been ill mate."

"Yeah, a bit, but I did also fuck her best mate, that hasn't helped much."

Tomo burst out laughing, "Fuck … you don't do things by halves do you? Well mate, I suppose every cloud, as they say."

"Yeah, but to be honest I'd rather not have done that."

"Sounds like you need cheering up. What are you doing now? Me and some of the fellows are going out on the razz."

"Nothing, just sitting in my car sulking at the moment."

Tomo laughed again, "Fucking poof! Come on, we're gonna meet at the Half Moon in the town for seven, then we're out to a club later if you fancy it."

"Yeah, sounds good, see you there."

"Later mate!" said Tomo and hung up. I wondered if I was doing the right thing, but I had nowhere else to go, so maybe, a night out would be just what I need.

#

I parked Adam's car in the local Waitrose , and quickly popped in to buy a toothbrush and toothpaste, and a can of anti-perspirant in order to have a quick freshen up before I went to find Adam's friends. I popped back to the car briefly and brushed Adam's teeth, swigging water to rinse his mouth out. For an instant, I winced at having to spit the water onto the street, but with a quick thought of *'Hey, I'm a bloke, who cares?'* I spat the water loudly onto the tarmac. Quickly squirting the antiperspirant under Adam's armpits and a quick douse over his clothes made me feel a tad more hygienic.

I have never met Tomo but found a couple of photographs on his Facebook account showing him and a group of other men in a pub. Tomo was a good looking man in his 30's with wavy blonde hair and a *Surfer Dude* dress sense. He should be easy to find I hoped.

The Half Moon pub was located in the old part of the town and was known locally as 'The Horn' a well-known venue for live music. I was very nervous as I entered and hesitated at the door when I saw the unexpectedly large crowd within, even though it was fairly early in the evening. I drew a long breath then stepped in amongst the throng of other customers. Looking around the pub, I could see a large mixed crowd of people standing near the bar area, plus others seated in the small seat areas around the outer walls and near the large Georgian windows. In another section, there was a rock band playing on a small stage area, with a few people standing at the front swaying to the music as the band made their first attempts to entertain. I stood staring at the lead singer when someone grabbed Adam's shoulders from behind. Looking around I saw who I immediately recognised as Tomo, grinning at me.

"You lost mate?" he yelled, attempting to talk over the loud music.

"Not now thanks," I said .

Tomo had a large infectious grin, and a warm friendly persona. He threw an arm over Adam's shoulders and led me to the rear of the bar where there were several seats and a long bench against a leather clad wall, where Tomo and his friends were sitting. Tomo made a brief introduction.

"These are my mates Adam and this boys is Adam. His wife has just chucked him out and he has a fucked up head, so we need to cheer his miserable arse up."

The friends were four young men of a similar age to Adam and Tomo. Each shook Adam's hand and introduced themselves.

The first was named Andy, a tall slim bespectacled man with short dark hair. Then Karl, a short slim fresh faced man, with a shaven head and the slightest trace of a thin goatee beard. Paul, a slim muscular sharp featured man, with close cropped hair, wearing a tight tee shirt which clung to his brawny torso. Finally there was Geoff, an extremely tall man with thick bushy hair shaven at the sides. He was dressed flamboyantly in a bright tight fitting flowered shirt, unbuttoned almost to his navel, complimented by skinny jeans high above his ankles, and soft grey sneakers. When I shook his hand, he smiled, staring deep into Adam's blue eyes.

"Oooh, hello Adam. Where has Tomo been hiding you?"

"OI! Hands off you letch! He's straight!" interjected Tomo.

"Shame, still the night is young," laughed Geoff.

"What are you drinking Adam?" said Tomo.

"I'll have a glass of red wine please."

"What? Fuck that! Have a fucking beer mate, we're on it! Stella okay?"

I nodded, although as Evette I was not a lager drinker, but I did not mind the odd mouthful when Adam drank it at home, so I went along with the suggestion. As Tomo was at the bar, I sat with the group, but I felt safest sitting next to Karl, who of the four appeared the meekest.

"So, are you still playing football Adam?" asked Karl, eager to strike up a conversation.

I hesitated slightly, as I did not often watch Adam play football, and knew very little about the game I did not want to get involved too deeply.

"Not so much, I've been a bit ill lately."

"Yeah, Tomo said something about that. You had a stroke or something, right?"

"Well, sort of.."

Geoff cut in, "Oh, don't start going on about boring football Karl. What I want to know is why your partner has chucked you out? Have you been a naughty boy Adam?"

I felt uncomfortable by the question, and could feel Adam's face redden, "No, nothing like that.."

"Ohh he's going red!" laughed Geoff loudly, "Come on Adam, you can tell us."

Strangely though, I felt a need to confess, if only to try and fit in.

"Well, I did shag her best mate, that might have had something to do with to it I suppose."

The comment brought a loud cackle from Geoff, and much hilarity from the others, and a brief session of back slapping from Karl.

"Good man!" laughed Karl, "if you going to shag someone, the best mate is the way to go!"

It was odd how the reaction was entirely different from a male perspective. If I had said the same sentence to my own friends, I would have certainly not been given any sort of approval. At best a few words of advice, but more likely some catty unfavourable opinion.

There followed a quick history from the others of lovers they had betrayed or cheated on, with much hilarity from the group. Despite my hidden disapproval with the subject of infidelity, I went along with the conversation.

Tomo soon returned with six pints of lager, and the evening begun. The conversation was mostly between the others, with the odd comment or question pointed to me, which I chose to agree with or try and answer vaguely without giving too much input. For some reason unbeknown to me, the group found me as Adam quite funny, and I felt more and more comfortable in their company. As the drinks flowed, the alcohol began overtake me, and the more at ease I became.

As the evening progressed, I found myself drawn more to Karl and Geoff than the others. Geoff because of his loud over the top Gay persona, and Karl for his friendly soft manner. The band playing live at the venue and the crowd of people dancing and enjoying the night really made me feel relaxed, and for once I felt happy in Adam's body. We had had taken turns buying rounds of drink when my turn came round again. Staggering to the bar I was now more than tipsy, but against my better judgement I found myself ordering a round of lager with the addition of six Jager bombs. The waitress looked at the slightly unsteady Adam as I slurred the words to her and struggled to tap my card on the pay machine.

"I'll bring them over," she said.

I realised that it was now a good time for Adam to pee, as the lager was making a determined effort to escape. Staggering to the toilet, I found it hard to control Adam's movements as I walked through the busy crowd. Usually as myself when drunk, I would have been all emotional, and crying at something someone had said, or thought about me in the past in a negative fashion, but as Adam, I was actually enjoying the out of control sensation.

Inside the toilet, I found the only cubical shut, so I had no option other than to stand and pee into the urinal, which was like an old metal cattle trough. The whole place smelt of urine, and I held Adam's nose with one hand as I struggled to pull his penis from his tight jeans.

'*This is disgusting.*' I thought.

A voice beside me made me jump as I fumbled inside Adam's fly.

"Do you want a hand with that Adam?"

It was Geoff, who had walked into the toilet behind me.

"No, I'm fine thanks," I giggled, "I am not used to pissing standing up."

Geoff laughed in a high pitched effeminate guffaw, "Me too! I can't stand pissing in a trough ! It's so disgusting! I do it the lady way."

"Me too," I said truthfully.

With no other choice available, I paid Geoff no further attention, and concentrated on the deed. Having released Adam's cock, I pee'd blissfully into the trough below. Due to the large amount of alcohol I had already consumed I found that I needed to support

Adam's body from unbalancing, so I placed a hand on the wall to keep me from falling forwards. Geoff had taken his spot next to me, and unbeknown to me at the time, he had a full and opportunist view of Adam's cock.

"I think you need both hands there Adam," he said.

Thinking Geoff was probably referring to my need to hold Adam straight as he pee'd, I gave no thought to what Geoff was really referring too, and what he was admiring. Once finished, I pushed Adam's bits into place, and staggered back to the group, leaving Geoff to finish.

Back at our table the drinks and the shots had arrived. "Come on Adam! We've been waiting," said Tomo. "Where's Geoff?"

"He was in the toilets."

"He didn't try and slip you one did he?" laughed Tomo. I just chuckled quietly, as Geoff appeared from the toilets.

"What are you saying" he called campily.

"We're saying did you try and fuck Adam in the dunny?" yelled Tomo over the loud music.

"Huh, more like him trying to fuck me! Eh Adam?" Geoff lifted the glass of Jager bomb and looked directly into Adam's eyes as he threw the drink back.

Oddly, I found his attention to be more than a little attractive. I lifted the glass of the RedBull and Jägermeister mix to the others crying "CHEERS BOYS!" The others followed suit, drinking the shots down quickly.

"Sambucas!" screamed Geoff loudly and pranced away to the bar to get a further round of shots. The band by this time had finished, and in moments the local D.J began to introduce himself over the microphone. Almost as soon as Geoff returned with the Sambuca shots, they were downed, and another set was purchased by another of our group.

By now the music was getting louder and the crowd livelier as the D.J played a string of 90's club anthems. In no time the dance floor was flooded with people, including me and my newfound friends. My mind was a blur. I had little control over Adam's body, or his insatiable thirst for Sambuca. I was totally engrossed in the music as I danced and jumped around with abandon. Then suddenly Tomo pulled me aside to stand between him and Geoff. Tomo looked about him quickly, and pulled a small ornate glass tube from which he produced a small spoon with a small amount of white powdered cocaine. He quickly sniffed the powder, then refilled the spoon and passed it to Geoff who did the same. Geoff then passed the spoon to me.

"That's not coke is it?" I slurred.

"Nah, course not," said Tomo, "Vitamin C, that's all mate. It'll clear your head."

I hesitated.

"Bang it!" cried Geoff in Adam's ear and pushed the spoon under his nose. "Go on you pussy!"

I could not resist; my mind was not capable. Snorting heavily, I sniffed the powder up Adam's nostrils. Immediately I felt the drug take effect on Adam's body. It almost seemed to sober him and me up. I felt euphoric, empowered, totally in control, and buzzing with confidence.

"Fuck!" I said.

"There you go!" laughed Geoff, "Now we're partying!"

"We need a club!" yelled Tomo to the others, "Are you coming Adam?"

I would now go along with anything; the alcohol and drugs had shaken off my usual inhibitions and I was totally out of control.

"Sure thing!" I yelled happily.

What could possibly go wrong?' I thought....

16

BUT HE'S NOT GAY.. HE'S NOT.

The Bachuss Club was the main venue for night entertainment in the town and just a few minutes walk from the Horn pub. It was now just past midnight, and after a short wait while the door staff checked us through, we were amongst a throng of dancing, partying 20 to 40 somethings, all enjoying the loud dance music. Tomo had rung ahead, as he knew some of the staff in the club well and had arranged a V.I.P table for us.

A waitress led us to our table and we were sat in a leather clad private booth. On the centre of our table was a tray of Vodka shots, and a huge ice filled bowl containing a bottle of spiced rum, and various mixers. Tomo quickly led the cheer as the first round of shots were drunk down quickly, followed by a Rum chaser. We chatted loudly as we surveyed the crowd, pointing at various girls and boys that caught our eyes. More shots, Rum and Red Bull drinks flowed. My mind was now a blur of alcoholic haze and euphoria as the cocktail of stimulant and alcohol bombarded Adam's body. I was very drunk, and I felt the need to stand before Adam's body crumpled.

"Come on! Let's dance!" I yelled, and pulled on Tomo and Geoff's arms, dragging them into the crowd of partiers. The music was a mix of modern and classic dance to suit the mixed crowd and I was loving the experience. As Evette, I had never let myself go as much as tonight and I danced like crazy, not giving a single thought as to how others would perceive a young man cavorting around like a drunken girl, screaming loudly.

The next song to play was '*Hips Don't Lie*' by *Shakira,* which was one of my favourites. I screamed loudly and grabbed Geoff to face me yelling "I love this!" I then began to gyrate Adam's hips around in a Latino dance made famous by the singer. I threw Adam's arms into the air, hands poised openly, and hips undulating up and down. I turned slowly in a half circle, lips pouting as Geoff emulated my every move. I had totally forgot that by appearances I was a man, and happily threw every piece of my remaining femininity into the dance, attracting many stares from on lookers.

Geoff made his way behind me, grasping Adam's gyrating hips from behind, and proceeded to grind his own hips against Adam's backside. To me, this felt perfectly acceptable in my drunken mind, and I gyrated around happily, eyes closed , waving Adams hands in the air rhythmically.

The D.J then played the track *Insomnia* by *Faithless*, "OH MY GOD! I LOVE THIS!" yelled Geoff, as the renowned dance tune introduction began to boom out. Much of the crowd reacted the same and began slowly swaying as the tune built to its famous crescendo. The flashing lights, the heavy dance beat, and the alcohol and cocaine blew my mind and Adam's body. I danced and jumped up and down as the music fired into a fast heavy beat, my mind totally lost in the ecstasy of the moment. But with each jump, I could feel Adam's body swaying and becoming more unbalanced. His resistance to the booze and drugs had peaked, and I needed to slow his body down, quickly.

I was now feeling dizzy, so I staggered from the dance floor and grabbed a side of a table for support. The strobe lights of the club were hypnotic, and as I stared around at the many faces, the apparent slowness of their movements made Adam's unbalanced state worsen. Suddenly I felt sick, very sick!

'Oh my God, I'm going to throw up!'

I staggered through the crowd towards the neon lit toilet sign, causing some offence as Adam's frame barged into several dancers across the floor. I first naturally attempted to enter the ladies toilet to a barrage of abuse from the queuing women clubbers waiting patiently for a free cubicle. I then felt someone grab Adam's shoulders from behind and found myself being guided towards the Gentlemen's toilets. Looking behind I saw the smiling face of Geoff coming to my rescue.

Pushing through the thankfully almost empty toilets I briefly looked into the slightly scornful eyes of what I assumed to be a toilet attendant, before I was hustled into a toilet cubicle, with Geoff at Adam's rear.

The sight of the toilet pan caused a huge surge to erupt from

Adam's abdomen, and I threw up heavily into the toilet. A disgusting dark liquid shot from Adam's mouth as his body retched loudly into the bowl. Half collapsing forwards, I felt Adam's knees fold as I grasped the sides of the toilet pan for support, allowing Adam's head to fall within the bowl as I continued to throw up. Once I had finished, I became aware that Geoff was still behind me and he began to rub Adam's back gently.

"Wait there Adam," he said softly. He left the cubicle briefly leaving me kneeling next to the toilet, sniffing, and trying to catch my breath. As I sniffed and took deep breaths to try and calm Adam's racing heart, I could hear Geoff talking to someone outside, explaining that Adam was ill. In a few seconds Geoff returned and bent down with a warm wet flannel and began to wash Adam's face, as I sat back against the wall of the cubical. I sat quietly, feeling slowly better after throwing up, and enjoying the comfort of Geoff's attentive care.

"Open your mouth," he said softly. I complied, opening Adam's mouth partially, allowing Geoff to squirt a small amount of mint flavoured breath freshener onto his tongue.

"Better?" he said smiling. I nodded.

"Come on, let's get you off this floor. Luckily for you the attendant keeps it clean, otherwise you'd be in a right mess!" laughed Geoff.

He helped me up, and again rubbed around Adam's face and mouth with the flannel. I was still very unsteady, and I was enjoying the help offered by Geoff. The music in the toilets suddenly rose in volume as the door was opened by someone outside but fell again as the door closed. Geoff was standing very close now, as he continued to gently pat the flannel around Adams face and chin. I found myself gazing into his eyes, enjoying his handsome comforting smile . I felt Geoff's hand under Adam's chin, as he pulled him closer, and before I knew it, I felt Geoff's soft lips lock against Adam's. I did not resist. It felt perfectly natural and free of any guilt. The embraced quickened, and I threw Adam's arms around Geoff's waist, and pulled him close. I felt Geoff's hands running up and down Adam's back, then down to his backside, clenching both of his bum cheeks firmly.

Geoff pulled his lips away, and kissed Adam around the side of his neck, as his hands ran around the front of Adam's jeans. Adam was erect, and although I began to think that I should not allow him to be touched in this way, I could not resist. Geoff then turned me around to face the wall, as he continued to undo Adam's belt and fly. He grasped Adam's hard cock from behind and began to masturbate him quickly. I just gave in completely. I placed both of Adam's hands against the toilet wall supporting him as I enjoyed the sensation in his loins.

'*But he's not Gay.. he's not!'* I kept thinking, but somehow I did not care. It felt good, it was what I needed. What Adam needed.

I felt Geoff grabbing the rear of Adam's jeans, and he began to ease them and his underpants down lower. Geoff was quietly speaking in Adam's ear, but I could not understand what he was saying, as he masturbated Adam faster and faster. I could feel Adam was close to climaxing, and I just wanted to cum, badly.

"I think I'm going to cum." I whispered.

"Not yet, wait Adam," said Geoff, and he slowed his pace on Adam's cock. I suddenly felt a hard pressure beneath Adam's crutch and around his anus, as Geoff then began to try and penetrate him from behind.

"Relax Adam, relax," said Geoff into Adam's ear.

"What ? NO! I don't want this." I said, becoming fully aware of Geoff's intentions.

"You do! It's alright Adam, just relax." Geoff made a firm push against Adam's backside, causing me to thrust Adam's hips forward to avoid it. I quickly turned away to face Geoff as I grabbed Adam's jeans and pulled them up abruptly.

"I fucking don't Geoff!" I barked loudly facing him.

At that point a man poked his head over the top of the cubical.

"Oi! I know what you're doing! Fucking queers!"

"Oh Fuck off!" shouted Geoff, and quickly unlocked the door, pushing past the man behind it. I was a little shocked by the sudden turn of events, and pushing the cubicle door closed again, I stayed a few moments as I gathered my thoughts. I took several breaths to calm Adam's body down, then made my decision to leave. The outer door during this time had opened and closed with the rise and fall of the music outside, so thinking that I was alone I slowly opened the door. Suddenly though the door was pushed back fully from outside, and a burly man in a dark suit abruptly pulled me from the cubicle.

“You! Out! This aint a fucking knocking shop!”

A second similarly dressed male stood behind the first. I recognised both as the door staff and realised that I was about to be ejected.

“Hang on, can I just let my friends know?”

“No, you’re leaving, now!”

I felt myself sobering quickly, and my natural defiance began to loom.

“How dare you! I want to see the manager!”

“No, you’re leaving now, or I’m gonna throw you out.”

I looked at the doorman. Although he was quite muscular, he was overweight, in his fifties at least, and in Adam, I did not feel that threatened by him. Furthermore, I could feel the testosterone build in Adam’s body as his fight or flight response began to kick in. I chose fight.

“Fuck off!” I growled.

“What?”

“Are you fucking deaf? I said, Fuck..” I paused, and pointed a finger at the doorman’s chest, “off!”

I poked the doorman hard in the chest, expecting him to back off. He didn’t.

The doorman’s reaction was instant, and over in a blur. I did not see the punch coming or feel it. It was just a strange noise between my ears, and a mixture of stars and spinning lights in my eyesight. I was then somehow floating above the ground, and I glided out of the toilets. Through Adam’s eyes I could see the club lights flashing around me and the shapes of numerous people from the waist up looking down on me, as I seemed to float through the crowd on my back. I was unaware of how I was managing to move through the club, until it was made clear to me when the doormen threw Adam’s body like a sack of coal onto the hard pavement outside.

“Now *you*.. fuck off!” said the doorman, before shutting the club door.

I slowly tried to stand but was unsteady and instead I crawled towards a nearby bollard. I sat leaning against it as I tried to assess the state of Adam’s body. I was still very drunk and found it hard to stand. Other people were leaving the club and hanging around outside, and I saw that I was getting unwelcome attention from the odd few. It was now obvious by their absence that Tomo and his friends were either unaware of my plight, or did not care. My only wish now, was to get away from there. I had to move. I felt in danger, I was scared and had to get home somehow.

Staggering to my feet, I took several steps in the general direction of where I had left Adam's car but fell over. The laughter of several on lookers filled my ears and the odd rebuke made me determined to get a grip. Steadying Adam's weight against another bollard, I rose to my feet, and began to walk slowly away from the crowd.

17

IT IS PRONOUNCED SAHARASRABUDHHE, AND YES I AM HE.

Once clear of the nightclub I began to feel slightly better, and I could just about control Adam's inebriated body enough to walk in the rough direction of Waitrose. Finally reaching the car, I fumbled in his jeans for the keys which thankfully were there intact. Slumping into the driver's seat, I breathed a sigh of relief. The car park was almost completely devoid of cars, so I felt relatively safe to try and sleep the alcohol off. Switching on the ignition, I started the engine in order to warm up the car in the chill of the night and reclined the seat back as far as I could. Closing Adam's eyes, I tried to sleep, but almost immediately the interior of the car began spinning.

God, I feel sick ..'

I flung open the car door and immediately 'threw up' onto the floor, retching and coughing loudly. Again and again I heaved as Adam's body purged out the evenings alcohol. I hung there half in and half out of the car, clinging on to the door armrest and doorway with each hand, groaning and moaning loudly. The lights of a car entering the car park partially illuminated the area, and I stared miserably at the distorted reflection of Adam's face in puddle of mostly liquid vomit. I groaned loudly as Adam's stomach tightened again and I began retching further, making an alarming cacophony of animal type howls and moans.

I felt almost completely disabled, barely able to haul myself back into the driver's seat. So I hung there, spitting and dribbling into my self made vomit puddle. Then, without warning, a large pair of boots arrived into my peripheral vision.

"Excuse me sir, are you ill or injured?" said the owner of the boots. I did not bother to look up, as I was too incapacitated to look above the floor.

"What?" I mumbled.

"Are you ill or injured?" the male owner of the boots repeated.

"No, I'm fucking pissed. Fuck off!"

The man did not answer but stepped forward and leant over me into the car, removing the keys. I lifted my gaze to see that he was wearing black trousers, and as I looked higher I took in a green Hi-Viz jacket, a thick black vest with numerous pouches and pockets, and the word POLICE emblazoned on the vest.

"Fuck.." I groaned.

"I am arresting you for … Fuck me.. Is that you Adam?"

I looked at the man's face, I instantly recognised him as one of our neighbours, Frank.

Thank God!

I was truly relieved to see my neighbour rather than a stranger, but somehow my situation oddly amused me, and instead of trying to show some control, I began giggling as I tried to address Frank, speaking in an idiotic off key melodic garble.

"Franky … Franky.. Frannn..keeee.. hello Frank, are you well? Have you come to rescue me?" I slurred.

Frank looked over his shoulder towards the Police car, then around the car park area. There were no persons nearby.

"You're wrecked," he said, "What there fuck are you doing?"

"I think someone has slipped me some drugs in a night club. A bloke tried to shag me." I found the conversation funny for some reason and I began giggling again.

"It's not funny Adam, what am I supposed to do with you? I should nick you mate you're so pissed."

"You could take me home…please?"

Frank paused, again looking around him in the car park. Aware of the layout of the local CCTV, he knew where the camera blind spots were. Fortunately for Adam they were positioned in one. To arrest Adam, rather than leave him would be the right thing but taking him home would be the better option for them both. Better for Adam so he would not be possibly banned from driving, and better for Frank that he avoids the paperwork and embarrassment that he arrested one of his neighbours.

Lifting Adam's giggling frame back into the car, he slapped his face gently twice. I looked into his eyes.

"Right Adam, here's what we are going to do. There's CCTV all over this car park, so I have to put you in the car. But I will take you home if.. and only if you ring me tomorrow and if anyone has reported your car or you, I will take a statement of this drink spiking thing. Do you understand?"

I nodded, the last thing I wanted was to have Adam arrested and banned from driving. Even in my drunken state I could see that Frank was doing us both a great favour.

Frank helped me from Adam's car and into the back of the police car. He began driving out when I remembered that my other self had thrown me out, and I could not bear to see her in this state.

"No wait Frank, you can't take me home. Evette has thrown me out."

"For Fuck sake..," he said irritably, " so where do you want to go?"

I could only think of one person, Mel.

"Can you take me to Epping way? My friend lives there."

I gave Frank the directions to Mel's house, and we chatted as he drove slowly through the quiet streets towards Epping. I began to explain the breakup, but as I spoke I got over emotional again and burst into tears. Frank did his best to talk, but from his short replies it seemed that he was just listening to the ramblings of a very drunk friend, and was probably beginning to wish he had left Adam in the car park.

I closed Adam's eyes and sat silently as we drove along a dark winding country road, and I started to drift off to sleep. Suddenly I was woken by the car radio crackling into life. I could not quite understand what was being said but caught the words Burglary and armed. Frank responded with a call sign, then suddenly sped up briefly before pulling up sharply outside an old church. He jumped from the car and went to the rear where I was sitting. Opening the door, he grabbed Adam's arm, and pulled me persuasively from the seat.

"Sorry mate, but you're on your own."

"What? Can't you take me to Mel's?"

"No, there's an aggravated burglary now. I've got to go. Sorry bud, call a cab."

"But.. it's dark! I'm scared!"

Frank laughed, "You'll be okay, ring a cab. Sorry but you're out of favours mate. Cheers."

With that, Frank jumped back into the police car, and sped away, blue lights flashing. I watched the lights disappear into the night, leaving me in total darkness.

"Frank! Come back!" I called, in a pathetic half whimper, as the lights faded into the distance. My initial shock rose to a anger, and I uncharacteristically yelled after Frank.

"I pay your fucking wages! Come back now! Copper! Pig!" I screamed loudly.

I watched the last glimmer of blue light fade completely as the pitch darkness enveloped me. I was in a quiet country road, next to an old church. That's all I knew. There were no lights anywhere, despite the clear night sky. There were no houses that I could see, and I had no idea where I was. I was lost, abandoned , alone once more.

Fumbling through Adam's jeans I grabbed his mobile, which thankfully had a small amount if charge left. I rang Mel's number but after a few rings it cut off. I tried again, but the same result occurred. *'She's pissed off with me..'*

I then tried to check google for a local cab number, but there was hardly any data signal, and all I could manage was a blank screen. I searched through Adam's contacts and to my relief I found a contact marked CAB. I rang the number which was answered by a gravelly voiced man after numerous rings.

"Boss Cabs"

"Oh hi, I wonder if you can help me. I need a cab to take me to Epping, near the high road."

"Yeah, where exactly?"

"I don't know the name of the road, but my friend lives there."

"Don't exactly help mate," said the controller, "where is the pickup?"

"Er.. that's just it, I don't know."

The controller paused silently, "You're not exactly helping mate."

"It's near a church."

"What church?"

"Er .. I don't know.."

"Are you taken the piss?"

"No, no no. The police dropped me off here,"

"Sorry pal!"

The cab controller rang off. I quickly redialled the number and again after numerous rings the same voice answered.

"Boss Cabs"

"Hello, sorry we got cut off."

"No I cut you off. So if you don't mind I have other customers."

I panicked, "No, no no no, please wait. I am sure I can find where I am, look I will pay by card first if you like so you won't lose out."

Searching in my pockets for Adam's debit card , something in the back pocket of his jeans fell onto the floor. Ignoring the item I started to read out the debit card numbers to the controller, but then paused half way and asked, "Er how much will this be?"

"One hundred pounds." he said flatly.

"One hundred pounds? You're joking."

"Two hundred now."

"What? Fuck off!"

"I tell you what mate.. save your money and fucking walk! Tosser!"

He hung up, and I stared at the phone in disbelief. Enraged, I raised the phone in to the air, looking at the ground preparing to smash it in anger. I then noticed a piece of card on the floor that I had dropped while retrieving the debit card from Adam's jeans. I picked it up from the floor, and opening the card, I saw a number handwritten on the back, and a series of letters and numbers. Assuming that it must have come from Frank, I rang the number, hoping that it was the cab company he spoke of. The phone answered after a few rings.

"Hello?"

"Oh, hi," I said , "Can you pick me up please?"

"What? Who is this?" The voice sounded like an Asian man.

"My name is Evette, no sorry… Adam? I don't exactly know where I am, but a policeman gave me your number and said you are a cab."

"No, I am a doctor."

"But your number is written here, and a car number I think, DR66SHA. Is that your car?"

"Yes, how did you know? Who is this? Are you the police?"

I was confused, and still heavily under the influence of drink. I stared at the card again through the darkness, holding the phone screen against it to see clearer.

"No, the police gave me the card, I think."

"What else is on the card?" said the voice.

I turned the card around, to see a hologram image on the centre of a blue woman, clothed in ornate Indian dress. Underneath were the words **'Rati, the Hindu Goddess of Love.'**

As I moved the card, the four slender arms of the Goddess moved slowly and gracefully up and down, and her eyes seemed to penetrate my gaze. The card colours changed and flashed from blue to gold brightly and hypnotically as I stared further into the eyes of the deity. Below this were the words:

'Dr Kumaran Sahasrabudhhe, BPsy (Hons) MA, BACP. M.D MRC Pysch.
Psychosexual therapist, Relationship Counsellor .
The Rivers Hospital Sawbridgeworth.'

"It's you!" I gasped.

"I'm sorry, what do you mean?"

"You're the doctor! You're him! You're the fucking doctor that started all this!"

"I'm sorry?"

"It's you, it's fucking you! Fuck.. FUCK!"

The voice went quiet for a few seconds, then he spoke.

"I think I know who you are sir, you hit my car earlier. I gave you my card for the accident, I recognise your use of excessive profanity."

"But you are him! You are Doctor Sa.. har…ra.." I slurred through Adam's drunken state. I could hardly believe what was happening.

' *Surely this was the Doctor I saw.'*

"It is pronounced Sahasrabudhhe, and yes I am he. But it is okay, my car was not damaged at all. It is fine, so goodbye."

I panicked , "No, no no wait, please wait.. please! Please!"

The phone fell silent for a few seconds, then the voice said softly, "I am here, how can I help?"

I felt faint and sat down against the church entrance gate. Taking a deep breath to calm down, I began to explain.

"My name is Evette Barker-McCardle. I came to see you earlier this week."

“I mean no offence, but you do not sound like someone called Evette.”

“ I wasn’t me, I was my wife then, after I saw you I changed.”

“That is good, if the change was for the better.”

“No, it wasn’t, I have changed into my husband. You have changed me.”

“I cannot do that, that is impossible.”

“You have, I don’t know how you did it, if you even did. But you said that I needed to understand Adam, and that I needed to see things from his perspective. Now that I have become him, I do. But I want him back, I want me back. I miss him.”

“Look sir, I am sorry, but I think you have mistaken me for someone else. I do not think I have seen you, either as your wife or yourself. But take my advice, if you want to see the other person’s point of view, maybe it is time that you saw it from your wife’s perspective also. You may see things clearer then.”

“No, wait. Please. I know this is crazy, I can hardly believe it myself, but I know that it happened, and I am sure that it was you. I just want you to know that it worked, I do understand Adam now, I do. I just want him back, please.”

“It’s late, you need to sleep.”

“No, Holy Doctor, please please please bring Adam back to me. “

“Go to sleep..”

“Please please. Make it all as it was.. please..”

“You are tired my friend, just sleep… sleep.. sleep…

18

HOW IS THIS GOING TO END

The phone begun ringing, and I woke with a start, I was freezing cold and still leaning against the old church gate. On the phone face I saw that it was now 3am and it was Mel who was ringing me. In my hand I still held the card, but when I turned it around it was now plain other than the car number and handwritten telephone number.

'Had I dreamt all that?"

I answered the phone. "Hello Mel?"

"Adam, thank God. I've been trying to ring you. I had about twenty missed calls from you. Are you okay?"

"I think so, I am really lost Mel. I got pissed out of my head, and now I'm in the middle of nowhere, by a church. Can you come and get me?"

I explained roughly where I was, and what the church looked like which Mel soon recognised. After twenty minutes, the Figaro drove into view. Mel threw open the passenger door, and I was relieved to climb in.

"You won't believe the night I've had Mel."

She laughed, "After the last couple of days I will believe anything. Have you spoken to Evette?"

"Not since she said Goodbye. She doesn't believe that I am her…"

Mel's mood suddenly deepened ,"Please Adam. Don't start that again."

"But…" I looked at my best friend, and then shook Adam's head.

'She doesn't believe me.. no one believes me.."

It was useless, the whole situation was impossible, and at that moment, things were best left unsaid. I sat in silence for the short journey to Mel's house. Once there, Mel let us in and made her way to the kitchen to make a coffee. I stood and waited in the middle of Mel's lounge, where above the fireplace was a large mirror, and I gazed at Adam's reflection. I stepped close to the mirror, and looked hard into his eyes, hoping to somehow see any part of my own being staring back. I noted Adam's sad appearance, he looked gaunt, worn, and miserable.

"How is this going to end Adam?" I said, "Please, please, please come back. If you are somehow holding me in you, please Adam, I am sorry, just let me go."

I could not hold back my emotions as I looked at the face of the man I loved but had possibly lost forever. Crying now, I pleaded with Adam's reflection.

"Adam, I know why you are like you are, I understand why you did the things you did. I can see it now; I can feel your needs… I just didn't understand what it was like for you."

"Are you alright Adam? Or.. is it Eve?"

I turned to see Mel standing behind me. She was holding two cups of coffee, but her hands were trembling, her face was taught with emotion. She quickly placed the cups onto the coffee table and ran to embrace Adam's body.

"I'm so sorry I ran away, I'm sorry I ignored you. I want to believe what has happened but it's too weird, I just ran when Evette caught us."

I hugged her close; she needed the embrace as much as me.

"No, please don't apologise, it should be me. I am sorry for dragging you into all of this fucked up mess."

We held each other for a couple of minutes before Mel said, "Coffee's getting cold, shall we sit?"

We sat together on Mel's sofa, and I slowly sipped the hot drink. The coffee was welcome, and for the first time since in a while I began to feel normal, as the effects of the drink and drugs had finally begun to subside.

We spoke for an hour about the last couple of days, about Evette, the mysterious doctor, Evette's mother, Cheryl, Adam's work, and me punching his boss. Through much of the conversation I felt that Mel was speaking to me as Evette, but she continued to refer to me as Adam, but I did not push the matter of my identity too far.

I went on to tell Mel about my night at the club, in particular about Geoff and the incident in the toilets, which Mel oddly seemed to find hilarious.

"Mel! It's not that funny!"

"Sorry Adam, or Evette should I say. But if what you say is true you have got to admit, it is funny."

"How is it?"

"Well, if as you believe that doctor has changed you into Adam, in one day you have managed to fuck Eve's best mate, suck her mum's tits,"

"I didn't do that!"

"Punch his boss,"

I laughed. "Yeah I did that.."

"You got him stoned, got him pissed, nearly got him bummed! Arrested, and finally you froze him almost to death!"

I laughed gently, but then I frowned as another possible cause of my transformation dawned on me.

"Do you think that maybe I have had some sort of stroke Mel? And that I am Adam but I am losing my mind. Maybe all this Dr Sara..asa.. whatever his name is, is my imagination or just some weird dream?"

"No, it can't be your dream, Evette definitely dreamt that one. She frigged herself off in the car park of the hospital over that!" giggled Mel.

"But when I was at the church, I thought I had rung him. It was so real, and he kind of hypnotised me over the phone, then I woke up and you were ringing."

"Look, all I know is both you and Eve have been as weird as fuck, so maybe you've both been hypnotised, or you're both on some dodgy drug trip. Either way Adam, it's five o'clock in the morning, and I need some fucking sleep. Shall I take you home?"

I nodded. It was all I wanted right now. I missed my life, my home and my bed.

"Can you just ring Evette for me? Break the ice so to speak. Explain that I have been ill and I am feeling better now."

Mel raised her eyebrows, "I'll try Evette, but you can be a strange bitch sometimes!"

I laughed, "Yes, we can be."

Mel went into the kitchen leaving me to sit alone as she spoke to my other self. She was on the phone for a long time, and although I wanted to listen in, I felt it better to stay and await the outcome. Mel's voice, though muffled was a mix of tones and emotions. At one stage I could hear anxiety, then anger, followed eventually by a quiet responding dialogue which I took as either my other self giving in, or Mel herself.

After a while, I heard Mel's voice grow louder, and her saying a series of "Byes" to my other self as she appeared at the kitchen door, holding up one thumb and smiling broadly. Hanging up the phone she grabbed the keys to her car, "We're on! " she said triumphantly, "To the Figaro!"

#

The journey from Mel's house to mine was only ten minutes, in the light dawn traffic. I felt exhausted, dirty and dishevelled. Although it had only been a day since I last saw Evette, I felt an overwhelming emotion coming over me as we neared the Church Langley estate. Oddly I felt that I was not going to see myself but somehow I was going to see Adam.

As we approached the house I could feel the excitement in Adam's body at seeing Evette too.

Were we starting to separate? Would I somehow leap into my own body if we embraced? Was this the end of this weird but somehow amazing adventure? Would I remember anything?

The Figaro stopped outside our house, and Mel turned to face me, "Are you ready?"

I hesitated, staring towards the front door which remained closed.

"I don't know, what if this isn't the end?"

"You're not going to know sitting here, that's for sure."

"What if this is a sort of dream? What if I can't remember being Adam? What's the point?"

"Look, Adam, Eve, or whatever you are right now. You need to go in there, you need to face it. Whatever happens it can't be any more fucked up than the last couple of days."

I nodded, "That's true," I laughed gently. "The first thing is to get through the door."

"If it helps Adam, Evette is also missing you. So come on.. fuck off out of my car."

Mel smiled, and hugged Adam fondly. "If this does somehow turn out to be some sort of mass cosmic dream we are having Adam, and we don't remember anything, you were a great shag!"

I laughed, "Thanks, you weren't too bad yourself, even though you were the first and probably only girl I have stuck my cock in."

I kissed Mel on the cheek, and then climbed out of the Figaro closing the door. With a quick toot on the horn Mel drove off rapidly leaving me standing looking at my front door. I took a deep breath, and strode up to the house, just as my other self opened the door from within. She stood back looking down at the floor, standing aside as I entered nervously. I went to speak but Evette did not wait. She threw herself into Adam's body, wrapping her arms around him tightly.

"I'm so sorry Adam, I've been a complete bitch."

I did not know what to say. I was not prepared for this as I was expecting Evette to rant and rave at me, rather than ask for forgiveness.

"Look Evette, you were just being you. You haven't done anything really, but I have fucked everything up." My emotions again began to take hold, and I could feel Adam's body shake as he began to cry.

"I really fucked up, what with Mel.."

"Shhh, Adam, it doesn't matter, I have spoken to Mel, she explained everything. We can get through this."

"It's not just that, I have probably lost my job, fucked up our marriage, ruined your friendship, and your mum will probably never speak to me again. I just want things to be the way they were before."

Evette looked at her husband and stroked his face. He looked tired, stressed, broken. '*I have done this to him, I am such a selfish bitch*' she thought.

She gently took his hand and led him up the stairs to their bedroom. She sat him down and undressed him fully. I just sat there watching her intently but quietly enjoying the therapeutic attention upon Adam.

"Wait there Adam, I'll run you a bath."

I remained as the bath was run fully, I laid back onto the bed and closed Adam's eyes momentarily, trying to decide what to do next.

'How is this going to end? How long am I going to remain in Adam? Is this my life now? Do I even want this life?'

Evette returned after preparing a hot scented bath with Himalayan Healing Bath salts and taking the fully naked Adam by the hand she guided me into the bath. She gently washed his hair and body, softly speaking occasionally and kissing his head.

"Wait there," she said, then left the bathroom as I closed my eyes and allowed Adam's head to lie back until the water lapped over his forehead . The sounds of the room began to change as a strange rhythmic beat began resounding through the water. I lifted Adam's ears clear of the water and opened his eyes to see Evette return to the side of the bath wearing her dressing gown.

"It's Indian Tantra music," she said, "I got Alexa to play it, it will help you relax."

I laid Adam's head back against the side of the bath and closed his eyes again. The scent of the bath salts relaxed his body and mind, I felt the stress of the past days ebb away gently as the music of Sitars washed gently over me. Evette began to gently stroke Adam's head, then his chest and stomach. I then became aware of a pressure to the right of me and looked up to see Evette begin to climb into the bath, straddling a leg either side of Adam's body. She slipped the dressing gown from her voluptuous frame and tossed it aside as she knelt down across Adam's torso. She kissed his mouth gently, and grabbed both of Adam's wrists, lifting his hands onto her large breasts.

I was surprised but not shocked, although being in a bath, being kissed by my own self was bizarre in every way, I was now used to bizarre! In fact, it felt completely natural. As we embraced I felt almost pulled into the kiss, it was so deep, so intense, so … loving.

I felt a hand on Adam's erection, as Evette pulled away from the kiss. I opened Adam's eyes and looked directly into her breasts, and eagerly sucked on each nipple as I was gently caressed.

"You don't have to do this Evette," I said.

"Hush Adam," was the only reply, as she pulled Adams cock into her. She gently straddled Adam's hips on her knees, moving up and down rhythmically as the Tantric sitar music boomed out.

The warmth of the water splashing up and down his neck and shoulders added to the multitude of sensations across Adam's body.

I could feel Adam thrusting powerfully into her as our passion rose with the sounds and smells of the room, and for a brief moment, I was back in the same intense passion that I remembered with Doctor Sahasrabudhhe. In my mind's eye I saw him, his brown eyes staring into mine, his dark hands caressing me all over. I opened Adam's eyes, but I was still in our bath looking at Evette, her eyes closed tightly, back arched in pleasure as Adam's powerful thrusts enveloped her.

'This is wonderful.." they thought.

Our minds as one, somewhere between heaven and ecstasy. I felt Adam's body begin to spasm as the music and drumming grew louder, faster, and more intense as I pushed deeper and harder into my other self. Our passion grew and grew, until I could hear us both screaming as we came together, the water in the bath lapping over the edge as the tsunami of euphoria erupted from us in a final, unified, prodigious climax.

Evette lay against Adam's body until their hearts slowed, and their endorphins ebbed away.

"Let's go to bed," she said, and slowly helped Adam from the bath drying him gently and guiding him into the comfort of the fresh cotton sheets. It was what Adam needed, so relaxed was his body now, that he fell into a deep sleep as he and Evette found their minds relaxed, and finally at ease.

#

Adam woke in the early hours of the morning. It was still dark, and he fumbled around looking for the clock. It was now three o'clock in the morning. *Strange.*

He had an urgent need for a pee, so he sat up, and in half sleep, he slouched across to the ensuite bathroom. He left the light off as usual so not to wake Evette and lifted the toilet lid. He realised that he was not wearing any underwear, so took his usual pose of half leaning against the opposing wall and began to pee. The splashing of his pee on the floor quickly woke him further, and in a panic he urgently reached down to adjust the trajectory of his stream but peed straight over his hand.

'*What the fuck!'*

Looking down, to his absolute horror, he could see that where his large usually erect penis would be, was now just a mass of thick wet pubic hair, and his attempts at finding his shrunken penis only resulted in the pee spraying through his fingers.

'What the fuck? My cock's dropped off! I'm dreaming!' he

thought, as he rapidly felt around his crutch, and looked down between his feet for his missing appendage.

Realising that this was not a dream he screamed aloud, "WHAT THE FUCK!" and grabbed handful after handful of toilet paper in an attempt to stem the flow from where his penis had fallen off.

Grabbing his pyjama top, he lifted it high to obtain the best view of his crutch, in an attempt to see exactly what had happened. But, to his absolute horror, he saw that his once muscular chest had now oddly grown and was swinging around beneath his line of sight. He screamed louder, but his voice sounded higher, and strange. Then he could hear Evette screaming too!

"FUCK! FUCK! HELP HELP! EVE FUCKING HELP!"

The door to the ensuite flew open, and the light suddenly lit the room.

"What the fuck are you doing Eve? You're pissing all over the floor!" cried Adam.

What? wait no... what? That's ME !!

"Thanks for reading. If you enjoyed this book, please consider leaving an honest review on your favourite store.

Until the next time..

Happy reading.

Dr Lubeet."

www.ingramcontent.com/pod-product-compliance
Lightning Source LLC
LaVergne TN
LVHW010611160826
845677LV00013B/3355
9798840038420